WARNING

This book contains sexually explicit scenes and adult language. It may be considered offensive to some readers. This book is for sale to adults ONLY.

* * * * * * * * * * * * * * * * * *

Please store your files wisely where they cannot be accessed by underage readers.

Please feel free to send me an email. Just know that these emails are filtered by my publisher. Good news is always welcome.

Miranda Mars - **Miranda_mars@awesomeauthors.org**

You might also want to check my blog for Updates and interesting info.
http://miranda-mars.awesomeauthors.org/

About the Publisher

4Fun Publishing, a member of **BLVNP Incorporated,** 340 S. Lemon #6200, Walnut CA 91789, info@blvnp.com / legal@blvnp.com
NOTE: Due to the highly emotional reaction of some people to works of erotic fiction, any email sent to the above address that contains foul language or religious references is automatically deleted by our anti-spam software and will not be seen. All other communications are welcome.

DISCLAIMER

Please don't be stupid and kill yourself. This book is a work of FICTION. Do not try any new sexual practice that you find in this book. It is fiction and not to be confused with reality. Neither the author nor the publisher or its associates assume any responsibility for any loss, injury, death or legal consequences resulting from acting on the contents in this book. Every character in this book is over 18 years of age. The author's opinions are not to be construed as the opinions of the publisher. The material in this book is for entertainment purposes ONLY. Enjoy.

I Never Kissed A Girl Before

THE LAURA AND SHONTAY CHRONICLES, PART 1

Miranda Mars

The Laura and Shontay Chronicles, Part 1

I Never Kissed
A Girl Before

Hot Lesbian Erotica

By: Miranda Mars

© **Miranda Mars 2015**
ISBN: 978-1-68030-319-3

Life could be tiring when you were fucking your brains out day and night, it seemed, with half a dozen beautiful women, and dying to do so with half a dozen others. You could miss some sleep.

Dragging a little on her way to her office Laura glimpsed a woman she had never seen before talking with some other employees in the Project Management department, through which Laura had to pass, and indeed did pass every morning. The woman was very tall and skinny, black, clearly of African descent, but not dark, more light caramel-colored, the tone of her smooth skin falling between rich milk chocolate and glowing tawny velvet. She was very tall and very skinny, at least two inches taller than Laura, taller than either Randi or Yvette by at least an inch.

She wore a light tan pants suit, glasses with very large frames, and had her hair pulled tightly back around her head, though in back in fell nearly to her shoulders in a long pony tail, such a rare hair style for a black woman. Her hair did not appear to be so-called 'good' hair, but it wasn't wiry or kinky either; it fell naturally, and swished attractively around her long neck when she moved her head.

Laura hardly realized she was staring until she caught herself. Don't stare, she said to herself. Remember Tamara. Tamara had wanted to carve her up for lunch for such blatant staring.

But this girl did not resemble Tamara. She was not stunningly beautiful like Tamara—few women were—but Laura could see that her face was very lovely behind the huge lenses of her glasses, her eyes quick and intelligent, her mouth expressive. Very even white teeth. High forehead. Laura realized, as she tried not to stare, that this girl resembled Deshona more than anyone, and not physically either. Deshona was short, petite. Randi called her 'that dwarf.' This girl was as tall and thin as a Masai princess, though not as dark.

The resemblance to Deshona was in her icy exterior. The tall woman Laura was watching exhibited a crisp, serious, deadly serious, no-nonsense demeanor that reminded her very much of Deshona. Oh god, the fire under the ice again! Laura thought, knowing how it was a magnet to her lust. After Laura had scratched the surface with Deshona, the woman had turned into a raving, insatiable little fuck-slut. But you didn't know she would turn out like that, Laura warned herself, as she watched the new girl. This one may be cold on the outside and freezing like dead winter on the inside. You better not even think of it.

Laura tried to turn her head away. Anyway, she's marvelously, shockingly skinny. I don't even know if Jonelle was ever that skinny. Skinny and cold and intense. Laura ripped her attention away, aware that it was very hard to stop staring at her.

She passed a person in the corridor whom she knew casually and, trying to appear only mildly curious, asked who the new person was, the thin, tall one with the glasses.

"She's the new Director of Project Management. Shontay something. I don't know her last name." The woman made a dour face. "She's looks to be all of twenty-five, right? I guess the sky's the limit if you're already a director at twenty-five."

Laura smiled tightly and moved on. There were other matters to encumber her day, but through it all her mind kept drifting back to . . . fire and ice. I wonder if she burns under that glacier, she thought. Oh well. You have enough trouble without that. Just keep your eyes to yourself.

But, in spite of her efforts, a few days later she actually got caught staring.

Passing a conference room shortly after lunch, one in which she often attended meetings herself, she saw the door ajar. Shontay was holding a meeting with some of her staff.

For some reason, Laura stopped. She couldn't take her eyes off the woman. It was a mesmerizing moment, and she wondered to herself, while staring, why she was doing it. Shontay was not really beautiful in any conventional sense, though she had the regal bearing of some tribal princess. She did not dress in an alluring style. In fact, she was very tall and shockingly skinny and wore severely cut business pants suits in drab colors, black or brown, that hung in billowy swaths of cloth over her bony frame. She wore her hair pulled tightly back in a bun, from which a long, charming pony tail swung, really the only endearingly human thing about her appearance.

(She did have a nice little rump, though, the kind that stuck out and up a little the way Laura liked, though right then she was sitting on it, perched on the edge of the table and haranguing the troops.)

Her smooth, light brown face was half-concealed behind huge, oversized glasses that made her resemble an insect, though Laura could quickly see that behind the lenses there was a very appealing and interesting face. However, the face turned coldly to Laura as she was staring. Shontay had felt her eyes, as people often did they were being looked at, though no one knew why. She glowered at Laura, who quickly looked away, feeling her face flush hotly as she turned and walked off.

Oh god, Laura thought. Oh shit, why did I do that?

She took some consolation in the fact that it wasn't as bad as when Tamara had caught her staring, and had promptly reproached her. But she had wanted to fuck Tamara, which Tamara had known. And, Laura now knew, Tamara had secretly relished the idea, somewhere in her secret being. But this Shontay Something was not even physically appealing to Laura. She was almost sexless, as well as imperious and condescending. I don't want to . . . do it with her, Laura reasoned. It's not the same as with Tamara. But why did I stop to stare at her?

For the next few days, she did everything she could to avoid the areas of the building where she knew she would be likely to encounter Shontay. At least she would give the woman time to forget what had happened. Maybe Shontay had forgotten it already. After all, Laura thought, I could've just been standing there abstracted, thinking, pondering something. She didn't have to think I was staring at her. I wasn't, really. It didn't really have anything to do with her. Maybe it was the sound of her voice or something.

***

A few weeks passed. At work Laura kept her distance from places where she might run into Shontay. No need to resurrect that little awkward moment of The Staring in the poor thing's mind. Sure, I looked. She is . . . intriguing. But I've got my plate full already. I don't want her. Anyway, she's . . . god, is she skinny!

But then, one evening as she returned from work and stopped to check her mailbox in the lobby, she was surprised to find, just closing and locking the mailbox a few spaces down from her own . . . Shontay Something.

They both recognized one another at once. It had been a few weeks since Shontay had caught Laura inadvertently staring at her, and Laura had taken pains since then to avoid any place where they might meet. And so, at this moment, it was very difficult for her to suppress a wildly embarrassing blush.

"Say, don't you work at Hanford Carpenter, down at 333 Market?" Shontay asked. She snapped her fingers, trying to remember. "Laura . . . Laura something, isn't it?"

Laura broke into a grin. "Well, at least we have the same name. Laura. Laura Robbins." She extended her hand. "I always think of you as 'Shontay Something'."

Shontay smiled. She was, for the moment at least, not nearly as icy and aloof as she often appeared at work. "Shontay Gibson."

She shook Laura's hand. Laura looked down at Shontay's graceful, beautifully-shaped hand. Shontay was not dark like Dawn or

Charise (or even as dark as Lila, over whom Laura had now been mooning for days) but more a rich caramel color, and her long fingers clasping Laura's hand were tapered and sinuous.

"Are you living here now?" Laura asked, now opening her own mailbox. "I mean, I've lived here for a while and never seen you before."

"Oh no," Shontay laughed and shook her head. "Apartment sitting. My parents live here. Ninth floor."

Laura's eyes widened. She had never felt so stupid. Of course. *Gibson.* "You're the *Gibsons'* daughter? They're in the apartment right above mine."

As soon as she said it, she wondered if she should have. Since Kendra and Jane had moved out and the Gibsons in, she had tried to be on her best behavior about making uncontrollable rutting noises with her girlfriends. But she knew she and Jane and probably a few others had let their guard fall a few times, and she had never known, of course, if anyone had been home in the Gibsons' apartment during those outbursts. For all she knew, they had told their daughter that a lesbian lived downstairs who was always screaming away in loud ecstasy with her various lovers.

She peered through the huge lenses of the oversized glasses that Shontay always wore, trying to see if there was some spark of recognition there. *Oh, the noisy lesbian!* Something like that. But she saw nothing but Shontay's light brown eyes, so pale brown that they looked almost green, very beautiful and in a way electric and alluring, though somewhat obscured by the glossy reflections glancing off the large lenses.

"What a coincidence," Shontay said, Laura thought somewhat uneasily.

Now Laura had collected her mail, and they walked slowly together toward the elevators. Though she had always found Shontay vaguely attractive, in spite of her painful thinness and her apparently very cold nature, Laura was relieved to find that she was not urgently drawn to the girl in any way and could leave well enough alone. Not such a good thing to be making a pass at your neighbor's daughter, she told herself. After all, you already did that once, with Jane. It so happens they lived in the same apartment. We will make sure history doesn't repeat itself this time.

Shontay of course helped matters by being almost wholly asexual. Today she was wearing her loose-hanging (because of her tall, bony frame) light brown business suit, in contrast to the identical black one she wore on alternate days. Once Laura had glimpsed her in an ivory-colored one, exactly the same. She seemed to have found one sexless garment and then cloned it in different drab colors until her closet was full.

Under the suit she wore a conservative white silk blouse, and around her throat a string of pearls. She had a long, exquisite neck. Actually, she looked elegant in a 'corporate' way. Today the pony tail she often wore, which seemed to soften her features and her aloofness a little, was absent, tucked up behind her head in a bun. Laura, incorrigible as ever, managed to sneak a peek at her cute little butt as they entered the elevator together and found it as wonderful as she remembered, high, jutting. She could, however, only imagine what it must really look like under the limp swaths of cloth that hid it.

Elevators made everyone uncomfortable, Laura knew. Shontay broke the silence, almost perfunctorily, gazing abstractedly up at the ceiling as she spoke.

"My mother has this cat. She's afraid it will be lonely. They're down in Mazatlan, at a conference and vacation add-on. So . . . I'm taking care of Willie, that's the cat. And staying there for a few days."

Laura was so glad, as the elevator reached the eighth floor, that she didn't feel a desperate urge to get into Shontay's pants. She's okay, but gosh is she skinny, she thought, repeating herself, as if chanting a soft, exculpatory mantra. She smiled at Shontay.

"Well, if I can be of any help, just let me know. I'll be right downstairs. You can even stamp on the floor to get my attention."

Shontay gave her a genuinely friendly grin, so friendly that Laura realized she herself must have been exaggerating the incident where she had thought Shontay had caught her staring. Maybe it had not even been noticed.

"I will. Take care."

Laura smiled as the elevator doors slid shut.

In her apartment, she promptly forgot about Shontay, feeling for once very proud of this demonstration of her self-mastery. Instead, she fell to thinking about Lila again, and Dawn. There was certainly enough emotional turmoil in her sex life to keep her occupied, and she didn't need to go falling again for that melt-the-ice-cube challenge she had already gone through with Deshona. She had not seen Deshona either for months now, and that brought her a fresh set of pains.

Reading her mail, drinking a glass of wine, watching a little of the news on TV, she lost track of time. When her phone rang, she reached for it distractedly.

"Is this Laura . . . Laura Robbins?"

She recognized Shontay's voice. "Yes. Shontay?"

"I didn't know how to spell your name. Whether it had one 'b' or two."

"Yes, it's me. Is something wrong?"

"Oh no. I was just . . . fixing something to eat. The idea of eating it all alone . . . or just with Willie . . . didn't seem too hot. I wondered if you wanted to come up and eat dinner here. You know, it's kind of lonely in this big old apartment."

Laura felt a tiny acceleration of the pulse in her neck. She had done her best not to think about Shontay in a sexual way, which was not hard since Shontay wasn't very attractive. Too skinny and remote. But now she could easily recognize a hot, feathery little excitement in her body that meant her interest was awakening. Could she turn the invitation down?

"I . . . haven't eaten yet. I guess I could," she heard herself saying.

"Good," Shontay sounded relieved. "I'll see you in a few seconds."

"Are we 'dressing' for dinner?" Laura joked, suddenly wondering if that sounded too risqué.

"Wear what you've got on. Willie won't care, and I won't notice."

"Be right there."

Laura went to the mirror and combed her hair and washed her face, so that she would appear more fresh and vibrant, feeling a little end-of-day fatigue. She blinked and scrutinized her eyes. Do I look like a sexual predator? she wondered. Well, I won't be. This is just a friendly dinner.

She tried on several causal smiles, then, dissatisfied with any of them, resolved to be warm, relaxed, and . . . what? Neighborly. At the last minute, before going out the door, she decided to bring along a bottle of wine.

Upstairs Shontay met her at the door, holding Willie in her arms. Willie was a white Persian, with startling pale blue eyes. She had changed out of the severe business suit and was now wearing black jeans and a faded red sweatshirt. She had removed the pearl necklace from her exquisite neck, too. Most noticeable to Laura, however, was the fact that Shontay's hair, always so primly combed and pulled back tightly, was now loose around her face, falling nearly to her shoulders.

Laura held out the wine. "My little contribution."

Shontay smiled, closing the door behind them. "Let's go see if we can find a corkscrew. My Mom and Dad don't drink." She raised her eyebrows sarcastically. "Their only vice is overwork."

They could not find one, and Laura had to go back downstairs to get one of hers. When she returned, they shared a glass of wine at sat by the window. The view was identical to Laura's but somehow seemed fresh, since the furniture was different, and she suddenly felt herself being attracted to Shontay in a way that she had not been before. She felt it even more so when Shontay removed her glasses, placing huge frames and lenses on a nearby lamp table and revealing a face that now seemed smaller, more proportional to the rest of her body, and very lovely, though still in a cold, remote way.

But now Laura could see her eyes better. They were light brown, almost green, and made her stare somehow electric and unusual.

"Why are you looking at me that way?" she asked Laura.

"Your eyes, I guess. I . . . don't think I noticed them, really, until you took off your glasses. They're stunning."

Shontay looked annoyed. "You think so? Maybe that's why I wear the glasses all the time."

"You don't like having beautiful eyes?"

Shontay gave her a curt smile. "They're odd. That's all. Big deal. How long have you been working at Hanford Carpenter?"

"About five years now."

"How can you stand it?"

Laura was mildly startled. Shontay was a newcomer to the company, but—as gossips had nastily asserted—she was only about twenty-five and had been hired in as a Director. It had taken Laura over four years to be made Director. Shontay was smart, attractive, aggressive, completely in charge, and could look forward to a very rewarding career.

She saw Laura's puzzlement.

"I mean, there's so much politics . . . so much devious political maneuvering. Don't you find it suffocating?"

This was always dangerous territory, talking with someone you barely knew about job politics.

"Oh, I guess I just wiggle my way through the sharks with a little smile that says 'Don't eat me, please'," Laura laughed uncomfortably.

"Do you mind if I smoke?" Shontay asked abruptly. "I mean, I'm not supposed to in their place, but if I air it out before they get back, maybe they won't know."

Laura smiled. "I don't mind. It's your neck, not mine. Your parents too."

Shontay crossed the room to her purse and took out a pack of cigarettes. Laura could not help letting her eyes linger on the girl's long legs and pretty ass, so much more apparent now that she was wearing jeans that fit her more tightly than the limp business suit pants had.

Again she marveled at how tall Shontay was. She was skinny-shanked, long, and lithe, but her curvaceous little rump stuck out when she walked.

After a brief trip to the kitchen for a saucer to use as an ashtray, Shontay returned and lit a cigarette with a brief, brusque, almost angry flourish. She was very angular and intense, Laura noticed. In fact, Laura had noticed it before, though only from a distance, and it had been one of the things that put her off. Now it only made her uncomfortable and wary.

"They hate it that I smoke," Shontay said, exhaling two long streams of smoke from her nostrils. "Anyway, I've only been there a few months, but I could sure tell you some of the sharks to avoid. Like that imperious bitch Rhonda Reardon for one." She looked at Laura for a reaction. "Maybe I shouldn't say anything," she said, looking away, taking a deep drag. "You and she are probably friends."

Laura was amused. "Did you have a little run-in with dear Rhonda?"

"What a cunt! Excuse me, I did it again."

"She and I are hardly friends," Laura said, delighted to have a way to ingratiate herself at Rhonda's expense. "She *is* a little hard to take sometimes."

If you only knew, darling Shontay, how she probably goes home at night and just dreams of pushing her face up between your long, skinny, brown thighs.

Shontay scowled. It was clear that just the thought of Rhonda about ruined her evening. That's fine, Laura thought, since I feel the same way. Let's change the subject.

They talked for a while about other things, but Shontay continued to be tense and sharp and her conversation full of treacherous angles that Laura preferred to avoid. After one glass of wine, they went to the kitchen, where Laura helped her make a salad. It was a small kitchen, identical to Laura's downstairs, and Laura was used to maneuvering around in it, but Shontay was not. While Laura was leaning down to replace something in the refrigerator, Shontay passed behind her, and when Laura stood, they collided.

"Oh shit!" Shontay said, dropping the knife she had been holding. "Look out!"

The tip of the knife grazed the knee of Laura's pants but did not cut through the cloth. The knife clattered to the floor. They both watched it, and when they looked up found themselves staring into each other's eyes, their faces very close, Shontay's hand on Laura's shoulder, and Laura's on Shontay's hip. For a moment it was as if they were caught in a freeze-frame, not moving, not breathing.

"Did it get you?" Shontay murmured the question.

"No," Laura murmured back.

Their eyes were locked. This girl is lovely, Laura found herself thinking, enchanted by the unusual soft billowing of hair around Shontay's face. She let her eyes drop to Shontay's mouth, which she purposely had not examined closely until now. Shontay's lips were full and curved and sensual. I want to kiss them, Laura thought. I want to devour them.

She looked back up into Shontay's mysterious pale brown eyes, hoping to see a warning there. *You'd better not try it*, something like that. But Shontay seemed paralyzed too.

Usually Laura had good self-control, but now she was unable to stop herself from leaning her head just a few inches more forward, tilting her face up—since Shontay was a good two inches taller than she—until her own lips brushed Shontay's. She moved her mouth slowly back and forth, letting their lips brush but not actually kissing the girl. Shontay did not move. Then she said,

"What are you doing?"

She did not raise her voice, but her stare did not flinch either. Laura stared back, trying to equal the steely force in Shontay's mesmerizing eyes. But it was very hard to control her anxiety at having made a huge mistake.

"I . . . don't know," she said, her outward calm concealing a wild turbulence inside. She pulled her head back. "I just . . . wanted to. Something about you just made me want to."

Shontay had not smiled throughout the encounter. She still did not smile. Her face was cold and suspicious. Finally, she seemed to relax a little, dropping her shoulders, which neither of them had realized were elevated until she lowered them. Laura realized that she too was tense and tried to relax.

Shontay bent down to pick up the knife. "So . . . you like girls?"

Laura's eyes were on the knife. Shontay saw her looking at it. A large, uncontrollable grin spread over her face.

She lay the knife down on the butcher block table next to them. "Don't worry," she half-laughed, "it's safe to tell me. Nothing worth killing over."

Laura played nervously with her fingers, smiling back now. "I'm sorry. I apologize. Something about the moment . . . I was looking into those wonderful eyes of yours . . . and we were so close . . . I could smell your perfume . . . I just gave in to the impulse."

A flicker of amusement and pleasure now began to dance in Shontay's eyes. She, like anyone, enjoyed being praised, enjoyed the thought that something about her had been irresistible to Laura. But she felt the need to taunt Laura further.

"You didn't answer my question."

Laura could see the steel flashing again. "Now I see why they made you a director when you were hired."

"Well, it wasn't any affirmative action bullshit, if that's what you're implying," Shontay snapped.

Laura was floored. "I wasn't implying anything. I think you're very . . . self-possessed."

She turned and walked out of the kitchen. You and Rhonda would be a good match, she thought, trying to get control of her feelings. Two of a kind.

Momentarily, but not immediately, Shontay followed her. She seemed conciliatory. Laura was gazing out the window at the view, the same one she could see from her own apartment. She acted as if she were alone when Shontay joined her there.

They both looked at the view, silently. They could hear one another's breathing.

"You don't have to answer it," Shontay finally said, softly.

Laura turned to her. "I . . . just wanted to do it," she repeated. "I couldn't help it. I can go now, if you like."

Shontay looked down, embarrassed, and Laura suddenly realized that the girl had been excited by the brushing of their lips, and she didn't want Laura to go but didn't know how to say otherwise.

"I . . . I can't eat all that salad myself," she half-whispered. "It'll just get rotten. Willie doesn't eat salad." She grinned.

Suddenly, and for the first time, Laura felt an overpowering lust for Shontay, a true, hot, physical craving for her body, painfully skinny though it might be. She wanted to enfold the girl, and break through the ice shield into the quivering vulnerability inside. If I stay, Laura thought, I won't be able to ignore this feeling. Better to let it all out at once, better to risk it now than later.

"I want to do that again. What we did in the kitchen," she said softly, boldly, letting her eyes dive deep into Shontay's pale brown miracles.

Shontay shook her head ever so slightly. "I don't think so."

"Why not?"

Now Shontay's embarrassed look became even more acute. She realized it and turned away from Laura, even moving a few steps back from the window.

"I just . . . don't go for it is all. I just don't do that. With men either. It's just not my thing."

Laura pursued her. She felt that she had no choice, and she moved a few more steps toward Shontay. Finally she was as close to her as they had been by the window. Laura reached out and caressed her smooth light brown cheek.

"Your skin is so smooth," she whispered.

She let her finger move around to Shontay's mouth, turning it so that the knuckle slid tenderly across the girl's sensual lips. Shontay seemed hypnotized by this tenderness, which was exactly Laura's intent. She could almost feel the yearning inside the girl, fighting to get out of the ice cage that entrapped it.

Abruptly, Shontay turned her head away, then turned her whole body and walked away without a word, returning to the kitchen. Laura did not follow her. She needs to be alone with those feelings for a minute, she reasoned. Whatever they are. Laura found Willie and began stroking him, making friends. Willie purred like a love-starved tractor and rubbed the side of his head violently against Laura's hand.

After a few minutes had passed, she went into the kitchen. It was remarkable how not talking, not facing one another for a brief interval could alter the mood again. Shontay was brisk and indifferent, as if Laura had never brushed her lips with her own. Laura fell right into the mood and picked up the salad bowl, moving it to the small dining table on the other side of the counter top.

"Another glass of wine?" she asked.

Shontay smiled. It was a very different smile from any she had given Laura before, somehow more intimate, warmer. We kissed, Laura thought. It was only a little brush of the lips, but she knows we kissed. That's what she's smiling about.

She poured each of them another glass of wine. Shontay had still not moved from the kitchen toward the table. Laura waited. Shontay turned and looked at her.

"You really want to do that again?" she asked, so softly that Laura almost could not hear her.

Laura's heart fluttered. Yes!

She walked calmly around the counter and back into the kitchen. "Yes," she whispered, looking dreamily up into the electrifying pale brown eyes. "But you're so tall . . . you'll have to stoop down a little."

"I don't mind that," Shontay whispered back. "No touching, though."

"No touching," Laura shook her head.

Their eyes were locked in a pulsing connection as they brought their faces close, then closer. Shontay bent her head down slightly. Their lips brushed again, as before. As promised, Laura kept her hands at her sides, letting her lips express everything she felt. First she lightly brushed Shontay's with them as before.

Their eyes were still open, still looking at each other, though too close to really see anything but skin and facial contours. Laura could almost taste Shontay's sweet, moist breath. Shontay did little but let Laura's lips caress hers. She didn't move or blink.

Laura slowly pressed closer. She pressed her lips into Shontay's marvelously sensual mouth, tilting her head to let them curve naturally into the receptive curvature of Shontay's own lips, finally feeling a slow awakening, a responsive movement in Shontay's mouth against hers. Now they were really kissing, not flirting with it, and Laura saw Shontay's eyelids fall, feeling an almost palpable warmth that had not been there before begin to radiate between their bodies, which were still separated by about six inches.

Moved and aroused by this warmth, and by Shontay's pliant, yielding mouth, Laura barely realized that she had raised her hand and let her fingertips run very gently across Shontay's cheek. But Shontay opened her eyes.

"No touching," she said softly. "You promised."

Laura dropped her hand. "You're right. I did. I forgot."

Now they had broken off the kiss and needed to start it again. Shontay looked at Laura, unwilling to resume it herself. Laura smiled and moved her mouth back into the position it had occupied when Shontay had spoken, now for the first time flicking just the tip of her tongue into the crease formed by Shontay's closed lips. Surprisingly,

Shontay parted them a little, not enough to let Laura's tongue slip inside, but enough to encourage her.

Ever patient, her hot blood beginning to surge through her body, Laura teased Shontay's half-parted lips with the tip of her tongue, expressively moving her mouth against them too. She tried to communicate telepathically with the girl, beaming her feelings at Shontay, reassuring her, verbally caressing her too, but silently. *I think you are so lovely, Shontay . . . so much lovelier than I had thought . . . so soft and luminous now with your hair down around your face . . . so afraid of a little warmth and so scared of your feelings. I would just love to kiss every bit of you . . . all of your long, smooth body. Wouldn't you like me to do that? Wouldn't you like me, for example, to kiss you between your thighs? Wouldn't you like me to kiss that pretty little bottom of yours? Would you let me? I could make you feel so good.*

This kiss had now gone on quite a while, and Laura marveled that neither of them grew impatient enough to push it further, or in Shontay's case, perhaps, to break it off. *She likes it*, Laura realized. She pushed a little harder with her tongue, trying to get it inside Shontay's mouth. Almost imperceptibly, Shontay's full lips parted more, then even more, and soon Laura's tongue was sliding in past her teeth.

This was a penetration of sorts, and both of them knew it. Laura could even feel a faint, very faint shudder in Shontay as she felt Laura's tongue enter her mouth. Her own tongue did not meet Laura's. Passive and yielding, she did nothing to stop Laura's probing tongue, though Laura could feel her breathing accelerate.

After about half a minute, Shontay slowly pulled back, breaking off the kiss. She was breathing more heavily, her eyes slightly glassy. She gave Laura a tight, nervous smile.

"I liked that," Laura breathed, smiling back. "Let's sit down and do some more of it."

Without nodding or making any other sign of assent, Shontay walked slowly into the living room, with Laura following. They sat down together on the sofa. Now Shontay's mysterious pale brown eyes were glowing, throbbing, dreamy.

Laura raised a tentative hand, as if to caress her smooth cheek again. "Still no touching?" she asked.

Shontay shook her head. "No touching," she croaked softly, betraying a physical excitement Laura knew she was trying to conceal.

Laura shrugged and smiled. "Okay."

As long as I can kiss you, I'll agree not to touch you. Laura leaned close, but this time before pressing her mouth into Shontay's, she let her lips skim the side of her cheek, then slid them down her jaw to her long, brown, swan's neck, so smooth and flawless. Laura kissed the delectable smooth column slowly, with great tenderness, down to the beautiful curved shallow indentation of Shontay's throat, then back up under her chin, until her lips again arrived at Shontay's mouth.

Now when they kissed again, even Shontay was more excited. She mingled her half-open lips with Laura's more ardently than before, letting Laura's tongue inside more quickly this time, even meeting it with her own. It became very hard for Laura to kiss her but not touch her.

"Can I touch you?" she panted softly.

"No," Shontay shook her head.

"Why?"

Laura kissed her neck again, the other side, waiting for an answer. Shontay was panting now, too. But she shook her head again with determination.

"I gave this up," she responded, after a moment's pause. "I mean, you know, sex."

She pulled back to look at Laura. Her eyes showed her sexual excitement, but her mouth was now pinched and cold and grim, the way Laura had often seen it at work. She looked exasperated, as if there were no way to get out of owing Laura an explanation, since they had gone at least this far.

"I never . . . liked it." She looked away, out the window. "So I quit. I've been happier since I gave it up."

Laura said nothing. She didn't know what to say. Shontay looked back to see Laura's puzzled, sympathetic expression.

"Never like this, of course. I never kissed a girl . . . until you. But guys, yes. A few. I'm so tall . . . a lot of them won't say 'boo' to me. But I did it . . . with a few tall guys. I never . . . really had a climax with any of them. And they were jerks. So I figured, why keep it up? I can be fine without it."

She gave Laura a tight smile.

"You never came at all?"

Shontay shook her head. "By myself . . ." her voice trailed off.

"By yourself you can?" Laura asked gently, trying not to be too pushy.

Shontay nodded.

Laura shrugged. "I love kissing you," she confessed softly. "We don't have to do anything else. You like it, don't you?"

Shontay grinned, embarrassed. She nodded. "I do."

"Let's do some more."

"Okay."

They had another long, expressive, exploratory kiss. Shontay allowed herself to get deeper into it this time, coiling tongues with Laura, kissing back. While they were kissing, Laura got an idea. She didn't spring it on Shontay immediately, being too overjoyed at this moving kiss, and Shontay's growing warmth. But when they stopped, she kissed Shontay's ear, her earlobe, her neck again, giving her the excited shivers.

"Ooohhhh . . . you're tickling me," she giggled.

"I have an idea. If you don't like it, just say so and we'll drop it." Laura smiled. "I'm enjoying this too much to stop it if you don't like my idea."

"What is it?"

Laura blushed a little even to say it. Her face suffused with rosey tinges, but her embarrassment seemed to charm Shontay, who leaned closer, as if to encourage her.

"Why don't we just lie down together and each do it ourselves? And we could kiss . . . we wouldn't have to touch any more than that. I'd really like to do it with you that way. I mean, it's not really like we're doing it. Just kissing, you know, while we do it alone."

This was very perverse reasoning, but Laura thought Shontay might be excited, and titillated, enough to swallow it. She might want to go through with it if Laura made it sound tempting enough. But Shontay just kept staring at her, as if in disbelief.

"How about it?" Laura prompted, losing hope quickly.

Shontay shook her head. "I gave it up," she said again, softly. "It's nothing against you. I . . . even like you."

She said it as if she could not understand why. Laura, in spite of the prohibition, again ran a fingertip along her cheek to her lips.

"May I keep kissing you?"

Shontay gave her the curt smile again. "Maybe we'd better not."

"One last kiss?"

Shontay tilted her head. Again her pleasure at being so sexually attractive to Laura was transparently obvious. She nodded.

This time their kiss, though it began slowly, became even hotter than the last one. Shontay was sending Laura very mixed messages. Not content to offer her open mouth to Laura, now she slid her own tongue back into Laura's mouth too, her lips searching, her tongue probing, her warm yearning very clear. It was an agony for Laura not to touch her as their mouths entangled in a hungry, aggressive kiss, hungrier by the moment.

Finally, they had to break it off before they incinerated one another. Both were half-dazed by the intensity of it. Shontay looked at Laura oddly, as she had before in the kitchen.

"You really want to do that?"

Laura smiled and nodded slowly. "I think I would come in only a few seconds if I were kissing you," she whispered, her eyes smoking with meaning.

"I . . . guess we could try it," Shontay said, tentatively.

Laura reached out and took her hand. Somehow it seemed to her as if they were moving under water as they slowly rose together from the sofa and walked in slow motion, still holding hands, toward the master bedroom. Since the floor plan of this apartment was identical to Laura's own, she could have found the bedroom in her sleep, and indeed it did seem as if she and Shontay were sleepwalking as they floated, glided, and sailed airily down the short hallway.

Only as they went through the doorway did Laura realize—and she knew Shontay did, too—that they were going to undergo this potentially marvelous experience in the bed of Shontay's parents. The bedroom, so familiar in its contours, felt at the same time very alien to Laura since it was furnished in a completely different taste, with golden draperies and French baroque furniture.

Fortunately, she and Shontay were still at least half-sunk in the sleepwalking mode, and together they peeled back the bedspread from the queen-sized bed, then turned on the small lamps on each bedstand. It was all so neat and clean and somehow elegant, and Laura could feel sexual excitement trembling deep inside her belly as she looked up to see Shontay's pale brown eyes glimmering and shiny, full of fascination mingled with a sexual allure that she probably didn't even know was there.

Laura went around to the other side of the bed and took her hand again. She encouraged Shontay to sit down on the edge of it with her, knowing how uncomfortable she must be, and knowing that they just couldn't stand there across from one another in Shontay's mother's bedroom and start stripping off their clothes.

"Lie back with me here and give me another kiss," she murmured, gently pulling Shontay down on the bed, face to face with her. "No touching," she added, partly as a little wry joke between them, which, Laura could see from the twinkle of her eye, Shontay caught.

They kissed, much more seriously now that they were lying together on a bed, where something definitely would happen. When they finally stopped, Shontay for the first time lifted her own hand to Laura's face and touched Laura's lips with her fingertip.

"How does it feel to have all that hair?" she asked, softly.

Laura had begun to unbutton the front of her own shirt, and she paused, sitting up, shaking her hair self-consciously. She remembered how, long ago, another girl had asked her the same question.

"Feels like I'm a lioness," she purred.

"Lionesses don't have manes," Shontay said. "The males do."

"Well . . . I'm not one of them," Laura said, finally undoing the last button.

Her shirt came open, revealing her black lace bra, cut low on her breasts, a very enticing one. She had not put it on specially for this but had worn it to work and just not removed it yet. But Shontay's eyes went to it immediately.

"No . . . you're not," she said.

Slowly, realizing this was a bargain, she began to pull her own faded red sweatshirt up over her head. Laura watched her smooth, rich, creamy caramel skin come into view, her lean stomach and waist, the nicely-defined cambers of her ribcage as she lifted the sweatshirt over her head and patted her hair back down. She wore a simple white bra, but Laura was delightfully surprised to see that it contained actual breasts, small but definitely there, round and bulging.

From looking at Shontay fully-clothed, you would have to guess that she was flat-chested, but actually she even had cleavage, and though very thin and a little bony, as Laura had expected, she was well-formed. The bones of her shoulders and her clavicles did not protrude in awkward angles but were sculptured and fine, and Laura realized that, though it might be a matter of taste, this thin, starved-model look was not totally without appeal. Shontay in only her bra was very lovely.

She also appeared more vulnerable to Laura than ever. Gone was the abrupt, sharp sarcasm and dour wit, even the aloof, remote scorn that was so apparent in her manner at work, and, even though she had moderated it, in her bearing when she had met Laura down at the mailboxes in the lobby. It was hard to be imperious and distant when you were in your underwear, about to share an intimate physical moment with someone you had never imagined you would do this with only an hour ago.

Laura smiled warmly at her. She unzipped her own jeans and began to slip out of them. As if hypnotized and only following the leader, Shontay began to do the same with her black jeans. Laura could not keep her eyes away from Shontay's long, skinny legs coming into view as the girl pulled her jeans down. She saw Laura's eyes on them and became self-conscious.

"My legs are pretty skinny," she apologized.

They *were* pretty skinny, Laura had to agree, and immensely long, but Laura found them very attractive, not really sticks of bone, as she had anticipated, but thin and shapely and smooth, with a glowing, almost mahogany sheen that made her want to press her lips to Shontay's shins, and her supple calves, and her elongated but satiny thighs. Oh god, I want to fuck you more than ever now, Laura thought, letting her eyes communicate it to Shontay since their eyes frequently locked and throbbed together.

"I think they're beautiful," Laura murmured. "If it weren't for 'no touching,' I would kiss them."

"You would?"

"Yes."

Now they both wore only their panties and their bras. Using both hands, Laura lifted her hair off her back, then turned it to Shontay.

"You help me . . . then I'll help you."

Shontay obediently unfastened Laura's bra. Laura slid the straps off her arms. She turned back, seeing Shontay's eyes fall to her naked breasts, then rise again quickly, as if she were unwilling to let Laura see that she was interested.

"Now you," Laura prompted softly.

Shontay looked at her, expressionless. After this garment was gone, there would be only one more apiece. Then they would be naked. Laura wondered if Shontay were having misgivings. On the other hand, when you had gone this far, it was hard to go back.

A small, ambiguous smile tugged up only one corner of Shontay's mouth. Her hair did not fall far enough to obscure her bra clasp, and so she merely turned her back to Laura and waited. It was an enchanting back, which Laura had not really seen until now. It was long, incredibly long, smooth, a rich, warm brown in color. I could spend a year just kissing this back, Laura realized as she slowly unfastened Shontay's bra. And she won't let me touch it.

Impetuously, she asked, in a soft, sultry murmur, trying not to seem too seductive. "Shontay . . . you have such a beautiful back. Are you sure I can't just touch it . . . or kiss it . . . just for a second?"

Shontay grinned back over her shoulder, as if she had known that once Laura had seen her back it would be endless love. Of course, Laura reflected, one rarely knew how beautiful one's back actually was, if indeed it was. Instead, Shontay was giving in to a coquettish impulse, of all things.

"You know the rules," Shontay said, eyes flashing with mischief.

Laura's face collapsed in disappointment. Shontay turned to her, slowly removing her own limp bra now. A subtle shift had taken place in her mood. She seemed delighted that Laura was so captivated by her body and was well aware that if Laura liked her legs and her back, she had a more surprising treat coming.

Shontay's small breasts were exquisite little round balls of firm flesh, not mere swellings, as Laura had expected, having slept with Jonelle, who had been surely as skinny as Shontay when they had first been together. They were small enough so that when she wore a silk blouse under a business suit, her chest appeared completely flat, but actually they were the size of tea cups, almost perfectly round, with soft, dark brown nipples the size of quarters, a slightly deeper shade of caramel from the rest of her lovely long body.

Laura was overcome by a craving to hold them, to kiss them, to suck them hungrily and make love to them painstakingly. And she knew Shontay could see it. Her expression said: *I knew you'd like these. See what I mean? It always surprises people that I've got these little gems.*

"God, they're beautiful," Laura said in a whisper.

Shontay looked down at her own naked breasts, feigning interest, as if her attention had been called to them for the first time. "You think so?"

Laura nodded.

"I wish I had bigger ones . . . like yours."

Laura could not suppress a giggle. It was rare that her breasts were bigger than anybody's. "Would it be 'touching' if we just . . . sort of, you know . . . pushed them together for a second? Just to see what it feels like?"

Shontay gave her another prim but coquettish smile. "I think we better stick to the rules."

But this time Laura could sense that Shontay now had acknowledged that this was a sort of game, and the outcome was still uncertain. Laura was willing to play along. Again she drew Shontay down beside her, face to face. They were still both wearing their panties.

"I want to kiss you again before we go on," she whispered.

Shontay smiled slowly. "I want you to know I'm really enjoying this," she half-breathed, very softly, almost inaudibly, as if hoping neither one of them would hear it.

"Good. Me too. I especially like kissing you. Your mouth is . . . so warm, so sweet. I love it."

Shontay squinted. "I kind of like yours too."

They kissed, very tenderly now. Again it was agony for Laura not to touch her. Shontay's tongue entered Laura's mouth this time before Laura had a chance to be first, and it made Laura's heart flutter all over again. She realized that she was very wet and wondered if Shontay was too. How could she not be? Laura thought. God, this is so exciting.

"You know, honey," she panted against Shontay's half-open lips, "if we don't get on with it, I think I'm going to come just from this."

Again Shontay was curious. "Really?"

Laura nodded. "I'm pretty wet. Aren't you?"

Shontay nodded. "Yes. Let's do it."

They disengaged their lips and slowly pulled their panties down and off. Their eyes never unlocked, and they could hear every rustle, every creak of the bed springs, every soft hiss of their naked skin sliding against the sheet, as they each slowly skimmed their panties down their legs and kicked them free of their ankles. Now they were completely naked, facing one another side by side on the bed, their mouths just inches apart.

Laura reached down with one hand to her crotch, parting her thighs, feeling the moisture in her pubic patch, the overflow from a wildly aroused cunt, which was throbbing and pulsing madly. Not wanting to be too obvious, she tried not to look directly as Shontay's hand descended too. Instead, she pushed her head forward again until her lips met Shontay's.

"Kiss me . . . Shontay," she breathed.

"Yes," Shontay sighed.

She bit her lower lip, and her eyes rolled up as she touched herself. Laura slid two fingers into the warm, buttery folds of her own pussy, feeling her whole body stream and glow with fire. Imperceptibly, almost as if they were sharing a dream, Laura could feel the whole atmosphere change as the two of them actually began to masturbate, slowly at first, but, in Laura's case, quickly accelerating. She wanted to go slowly, to give things a chance to develop, but as her tongue intermingled with Shontay's, and their hot, rapid breath filled the air around their searching mouths, she found herself rubbing her wet pussy more and more frantically, unable to stop herself from hurtling toward a thrilling climax.

"Oh!" she heard her own voice, softly gasping. "Oh! Oh . . . yes!"

Shontay's eyes rolled up again. Laura let her gaze travel down the girl's long, smooth, light-brown body. They stopped at Shontay's beautiful little breasts, the size of tea cups, jiggling and bouncing slightly now as she swirled her hand in her crotch, her deep caramel brown nipples winking out at Laura from behind Shontay's elbow or forearm as her arm moved. Oh god, I want her! Laura thought in a rush of desperate lust.

"Ummmm! Unnhhh!" Shontay groaned softly. "Laura . . ."

"Yes . . . yes, honey," Laura panted. "Oh, it's so good to do this with you. Kiss me!"

"Unhhh! Ohhhh!"

They writhed and squirmed, only inches from touching, their mouths moving hungrily together, their tongues dancing and stabbing more passionately now, their panting quickly modulating into an uncontrollable mewling as they both became more and more aroused. Breaking the rules, but almost without knowing it, Laura raised her free hand to Shontay's cheek, brushing back the black filaments of her soft hair and letting her fingertips graze the perfect, smooth skin.

"I want you . . . I want you," she panted, kissing Shontay more aggressively now, unable to hold herself back.

Shontay's pale brown eyes were now streaked by fierce sexual need, an expression Laura had never seen there before. She began to respond to Laura's feverish kissing more heatedly, opening her mouth wider, pushing her tongue further into Laura's mouth, whimpering now, writhing and shaking, moving her own hand faster, as Laura could tell from the way her elbow jumped and rotated.

"Oh . . . Jesus!" Shontay gasped, her eyelids fluttering.

"Shontay . . . I want you, I've got to touch you!" Laura panted. "You are so beautiful. Let me touch you . . . please!"

Shontay's eyes fluttered open, glassy, burning with sexual fever, telegraphing a message to Laura that all resistance was fading fast, that she was sinking and would not try to prevent anything Laura decided to do. Laura pressed her advantage quickly, not know how long it would be until either, or both, of them came. She pushed her face into Shontay's long, smooth neck, kissing and sucking it hungrily, nibbling the lobe of her ear.

"I want to lick your pussy," she whispered hotly, breathing into Shontay's ear while gently pushing her onto her back. "I want your beautiful pussy . . . let me have your beautiful pussy . . . please . . . please, Shontay."

"Oh Laura . . ."

By now Laura had slipped down to her wonderful little breasts, so perfectly round and firm, and was licking her thick caramel nipples, feeling them grow taut under her tongue, digging her fingers excitedly into the pretty round balls.

"I want to suck you," she panted, teasing Shontay's stiffening, saliva-wet nipples with the tip of her tongue, bringing hot little mewls of sexual delight from deep in the girl's throat.

"Oh Laura . . . please . . . ohhhh!" Shontay sighed, almost inaudibly.

Now, feeling Shontay yield to her caresses, Laura unleashed the full force of her passion, which she had been holding tightly in check for so long. She sucked one delectable, shiny, wet dark brown nipple into her mouth, trying to be gentle, not wanting to alarm Shontay by the full heat of her need, but unable to hold it all back. She sucked the thick, pulpy bud and pinched Shontay's other nipple with her fingers, sucking harder, until she could hear a reaction, a sharp, clotted intake of breath that told her she was on the right track. Shontay's body also clenched spasmodically, suddenly.

"Unhh!" she half-choked. "Oh . . . yes! Unhh!"

Laura was unrelenting. She switched to Shontay's other nipple, now twirling and pinching the wet, erect one with her fingers, devouring the second one with her mouth, sucking it hard, pinching it too with her lips. It was almost as if Laura, being so surprised and thrilled to find these marvelous little breasts where she expected nothing but a flat expanse of skin stretched over hard bone, was intent on sucking the beauties right down her throat.

But Shontay's reaction was not dismay; instead, having her nipples voraciously sucked by Laura in this way seemed to ignite whatever kindling in her body that was not yet burning. She keened and whimpered, rolling and surging and writhing and squirming wildly now under Laura, totally consumed by sexual needs Laura would never have guessed were there.

"Oh yes . . . oh yes!" she gasped, her eyelids fluttering open to watch as Laura squeezed and mouth-mauled her pretty little breasts, her head falling back to the mattress as Laura began quickly to descend lower, afraid that Shontay might even come before she had a chance to kiss her sweet pussy.

Shontay's body was long. Her legs were amazingly long, but her torso was long too, and Laura wanted to spend days just kissing the smooth, sleek, light-brown stretch of her lovely long stomach, so sleek and firm, her ribs a little more defined than most since she was so skinny, her hip bones protruding more, her belly smooth and deep. But Laura was also in a hurry, and she had to resign herself. Save it for later. I want her pussy, and I can smell it.

Shontay was so aroused that the thick, pungent odors of her excited pussy had begun to reach Laura's nose even as she had her mouth stuffed with the girl's delectable caramel nipples, and now, as she descended, the sweet, heady smells grew even thicker, and more erotic. Slipping between the girl's long, thin thighs, she came face to face with the small, gaping, swollen cleft of Shontay's open cunt.

Shontay had a small one, not long and sinuous like the rest of her body, but a modest little aperture, all runny and inviting with juices, the black inner lips puckered and protruding beyond the home provided by the outer folds, the inside a flaming, glistening magenta hole that beckoned Laura's tongue.

"Oh god, honey, it's so pretty," she murmured, spreading away with her thumbs the fibers of moist pubic hair that would get in the way of her tongue-rape.

"Ohhhnnn!" Shontay moaned, looking down her long body at Laura again.

Laura, peeking up over her black-fringed pubic bone, smiled warmly at her. "Are you going to come?" she whispered in a sultry whisper. "I'll bet I can make you come."

Though completely overpowered by sublimely urgent sexual needs, Shontay managed a frightened nod, like an entrapped deer, as if she had never come close to this feeling before. And of course, maybe she hadn't, Laura thought. Didn't she say she never came except by herself? Then this *is* completely new to her.

For some reason, this excited Laura further. It was like fucking a beautiful virgin, one who had thrown up every resistance she could think of but had been finally overcome by sheer dogged adoration and persistence, and the thrill was indescribable. Her thumbs, having spread away the stray hair, found the little hood at the top of Shontay's oozing pussy and pulled the skin back a little on each side, exposing the tiny nubbin of her clit.

It was really quite small, though proportional to the rest of her lovely small pussy, and Laura extended her tongue, touching the tip of it tenderly against the sensitive bud.

"Ungghhhh!" Shontay suddenly groaned, her head falling back again, and the lower part of her body quivering as unbearably sweet sensations shot through her. "Oh god!"

Laura was now in ninth heaven. "Does that feel good? Ummmm. Does that feel good, honey? How about this?"

Now she began licking Shontay's wet, inflamed pussy slowly and sensually, and since it was so small, it was no trouble for Laura to cover the entire slick, magenta blossom with nearly every stroke of her tongue.

"Unh! Ohnnn! Oh god . . . yes! Laura . . ." Shontay gasped, again holding her head up for a second, as if she could see what Laura was doing to her pussy.

"Oh . . . you are going to come so hard," Laura purred, now massaging the flesh on each side of Shontay's pussy as she licked it, again using her thumbs to pulled back the small hood, now tongue-flicking the tiny nubbin of Shontay's clit repeatedly, hearing the high, semi-hysterical whimpering that fought its way out of Shontay's throat.

Shontay was closer now than ever, but still she did not seem to have reached the point of no return. Laura had to concede that it was true, she probably was not an easy comer. God, I would have come about three times by now, she thought. I couldn't take much more of this.

But Shontay was quivering, moaning, twisting, looking down at Laura between her thighs, then letting her head flop back to the mattress, groaning, now undulating her hips in slow, rhythmic fuck motions. Laura knew she could bring her there, but it was a delicious challenge nonetheless. Thinking maybe a little penetration would help, she slid one long forefinger up into the warm, greasy channel of Shontay's cunt, twisting it and tonguing Shontay's swollen clit at the same time.

This seemed to ring Shontay's chimes, and the sexual tension she was feeling immediately seemed to jump up a notch. Her lovely long body flexed, writhing more violently, and the high-pitched, semi-hysterical moaning that seemed half-strangled in her throat became more desperate.

"Hhnnneeee . . . hnnneeee!" she gurgled, now digging her sharp elbows into the mattress and arching her back, quivering so wildly that her wonderful little breasts jiggled and rolled, making Laura want to mouth-maul them again, even though she was heavily involved in her present task. "Hhhnnnneeeee . . . oh god . . . oh god!" Shontay gasped, churning desperately.

"Oh baby . . . oh baby!" Laura purred back to her, redoubling her loving passion.

You *are* going to come, you *are*. I'm going to make you come, I know I can do it.

But Shontay seemed to have reached the breaking point. Her body was so tense, so raw and knotted with unreleased sexual frenzy, that she was shaking uncontrollably, cawing and gurgling in the grip of a frantic desperation, hungering so urgently for an orgasm that tears were actually leaking from the corners of her eyes as she thrashed and clenched and squirmed, trying to come. Then, with shocking suddenness, she collapsed, completely limp, slumping back to the mattress.

"Oh god . . . I can't!" she cried out softly, a wail more than a cry.

Laura looked up and saw that Shontay's face was now slick with tears. Overcome by concern and tenderness, she immediately slid up, enfolding her in her arms, kissing her fervently, warmly, fondling her delicious little breasts with her hands, cooing to her reassuringly.

"Oh, you can . . . you can," she murmured, kissing the tears from Shontay's shiny cheeks, kissing her eyelids. "You can . . . but you're trying too hard."

Shontay gave her a wan, bleak smile, blinking, her eyelashes bejeweled with tears.

Laura kissed her incredibly long neck again, nibbling her earlobe, breathing hotly into her ear. "Didn't it feel good?"

"Oh . . . god yes," Shontay gasped in a vulnerable, faraway voice. "It was . . . heaven."

Laura kissed her lips, a long, lingering kiss that rose in a simmering crescendo to a very fevered pitch. At first Shontay was again reluctant to open her mouth, but soon she was coiling tongues and writhing under Laura as heatedly as before.

"Now you just relax and leave everything to Laura," Laura purred to her. "Just don't try . . . just let it happen, okay?"

With a fetching sniffle, Shontay nodded. Laura slid down her long, smooth, light brown body again and resumed her attentions to Shontay's pretty little pussy, now puffy and glimmering with juices, all soupy and tangy to the taste. Again she slid her finger into it, feeling Shontay jump slightly, hearing a tight, excited gasp. Now, when Laura's tongue began to stroke her clit, Shontay began to moan in a distant, rhapsodic way, as if she were being transported into a realm of the senses she had always feared and desired but never experienced before.

Her moans were soft, but as Laura gradually accelerated the tempo, they became transformed into keening groans and deep, guttural whimpers. Laura knew she was on the right road this time. Oh yes, you're going to do it now, honey. You're going to surprise yourself. Come on . . . come on, just a little farther . . . a little more.

Laura realized, as she had moments ago acknowledged to herself, that she too was about to come. She had never had the kind of difficulty Shontay was having, and by now she could feel the overflow of juice in her crotch. Her pussy was throbbing like a fire alarm. Almost instinctively, she reached down to stroke it with her hand, wanting to get her own body into rhythm with Shontay's, since she knew the girl was about to come. Shontay's orgasm would be enough to trigger her own, she knew.

"Ohhnnnnn! Ohnnnnn god! Oh . . . Jesus!" Shontay moaned, twisting, raising her own hands to her swirling, naked breasts for the first time, pulling her nipples, now churning her pelvis in constant, even circles into Laura's face, clearly more wildly aroused than she had been even moments ago, when she had approached the pinnacle and then turned back.

"Mmmm," Laura hummed happily, massaging her own throbbing clit, now sucking Shontay's cleverly in persistent, rhythmic sucks, bringing the girl to the absolute inescapable brink.

"Oh . . . Laura, I think—" she suddenly gasped. "Oh! Oh, yes!"

Laura's hand moved faster in her own groin. "Yes! Yes, honey! Go for it! Unhhh! Oh god . . . me too!"

"Anngghhh! Ohngg! Unh! Unh!" Shontay began panting frantically, her moans now constricted into tight, hysterical little squeaks as she was sucked up into an inevitable crushing finish.

Laura, in the back of her brain cursing her bad timing, actually began to come before Shontay did. She could feel the molten honeyfire begin flooding her body, feel her muscles contracting and her toes curling, feel the birth of a throbbing star deep inside her belly followed by wrenching spasms as she began to be swallowed by it. Shontay, on the other hand, clenched, and clenched, her long, sleek body straining, her knees twitching up and to the sides spastically, her face seized by a terrible, agonizing rapture, and suddenly dissolved into a shuddering, mewling wreck as a huge, inundating orgasm engulfed her.

At first she made no sound but a raw, choked cawing in her throat. Then a low, keening moan seemed to travel up from deep in her body to her mouth.

"Unnhhhhoowwwnnooaauunnggghhhh!" she moaned, starting softly but then erupting in a loud cry that reminded Laura of how cats sounded when they were doing it.

Once this cry was out, a flood of wild squeals and groans escaped from her lips as her body began to thrash and quiver with each successive wave of her orgasm.

"Unhh! Auungghhhh! Oh . . . oh yes! Mmmnngggeeeee! Auuggnnhhh!" she groaned, coming in fierce bursts, her body almost shattered by each sharp, rupturing spasm.

Laura, though her own orgasm had not approached this intensity, was still half-crippled from the sweet spasms that were only now beginning to subside in her body. She slid up to embrace Shontay, feeling the heat that both of them were generating as it wound around their two naked bodies like a hot sheet, linking them together in a warm, throbbing union of sweet coming that took another thirty seconds or so to finally fade. Even then, Shontay was thrilled by four or five aftershocks that seemed to paralyze her as she stared dreamily into Laura's eyes.

"Unhhh! Oh god . . . there's another one!" she gasped, burrowing her face into Laura's shoulder and shuddering until it passed.

Laura simply held her, without speaking, stroking her long, smooth, naked back with her fingertips as Shontay suffered through the excruciating delights of this stupendous climax. They clung together for about five minutes. When it was over, Laura noticed that Shontay's cheeks were still damp, and she daubed them dry with the edge of the sheet.

"I guess that wasn't anything to cry over, was it," she murmured with a warm grin.

Shontay smiled back, suddenly bashful, so charming in a woman who often seemed like an ice sculpture. She shook her head. "I . . . never . . ."

But she couldn't get it out.

Laura kissed her mouth. "I know you never. Now you have."

"What about you?"

"I did it the way we first planned. You were too . . . busy to hear me groaning and gasping, that's all."

Shontay's brow knitted up. Her pale brown eyes, so electric moments ago, but now clear glowing pools, showed her deep concern. "But that's not right. I mean, you got me there. Boy, did you ever get me there." She made a funny face. "I don't think I've ever been there before." She paused, still scrutinizing Laura's face with concern, as if Laura were somehow still bottled up and ready to pop. "It's really not fair for me not to help you get there too."

Laura smiled wryly. "I'd sure like to go where you went. Looked like it felt good."

Shontay smiled, embarrassed. "You watched me. I feel kind of shy now."

"No need. You were beautiful."

Shontay's brow was still knitted. Without another word, she slid down Laura's body, pushing apart Laura's thighs with both hands. She remained silent, but Laura could almost feel her stare, even though she couldn't see her face.

"Laura . . . I didn't know what you meant when you said that about mine . . . but yours is really . . . lovely too. I didn't know it would be so pretty . . . so curvy and pink. It's like a seashell."

"Unhh!" Laura gasped, feeling a hot arrow of pleasure shoot through her whole body as Shontay's tongue first touched her pussy.

"Oh . . . I didn't do it wrong, did I?"

"You're doing it . . . just perfectly," Laura panted, falling back, parting her thighs further. "Yes. Oh yes! Unhhh!"

About a minute passed while Shontay patiently explored Laura's tingling wet pussy with her tongue, going at it tentatively but not shyly, determined to reward Laura for the stunning experience she herself had just had. She was unsmiling, very serious, as her face appeared for a moment above Laura's pubic mound.

"I even like the taste," she said, grinning suddenly, delightedly.

Then her head dropped again, and Laura moaned as the sensations grew more and more urgent. Her first orgasm had merely been a byproduct of Shontay's thrilling seizure, a little like yawning when you saw someone else doing it, but this time Laura gave it her full attention. And though Shontay was not very experienced, she was very ardent and deliberate. In about a minute, Laura was groaning and shuddering through a sweet and powerful climax that made her first one seem like an accidental sneeze.

Shontay patiently waited for Laura to recover her senses, which took a few minutes, before smiling and looking self-satisfied. "You do it pretty easily," she said softly, seriously. "Wish I could do that."

Laura had finally regained her breath. She put a finger on Shontay's wonderful, sensual lips. "It only takes a little practice."

She didn't know if she might not be lying, though. Some women might never climax with ease. It might always be a little harder for Shontay than for her.

At this moment, Willie leapt up onto the bed and quickly jumped between them. He looked half-astonished, it seemed, at both of them, then began to purr loudly. Laura and Shontay laughed and began to pet him.

"Hello, Willie," Shontay said, scratching him behind the ears. "Don't you wish you could do what we just did? Laura just did something to me nobody else ever did."

Willie licked Shontay's long brown arm.

Laura winked at her. "I think Willie better watch his step. I'm getting jealous."

Shontay looked askance at Laura, half-embarrassed again. She knew what Laura was talking about. Their relationship was irreversibly altered now. No going back. They had fucked, heatedly. They would doubtless do it again, and again, in coming days and weeks. Where there had been distance and suspicion, there now was intimacy. Oh god, Laura thought, seeing the expression on Shontay's face, which reminded her so much of Lila, of Tamara, of the others who were so afraid of what they had done at this moment.

But instead of dwelling on this thought, Shontay brightened again almost immediately. "Do you think we could . . . do that again?" she asked, almost shyly, looking down at her hand on Willie's fur so she would not have to meet Laura's eyes. Then she quickly looked up. "I mean, after we rest a little, you know. Not right away."

"Mmmmm, what's the matter with right away?" Laura asked, reaching across Willie to caress her face, letting her hand fall to Shontay's naked breasts.

By now Willie was truly in the way, between them, and he seemed to know it. With the instinctive escapist skill of cats, he speedily leaped over Shontay's long legs and bounded off the bed onto the floor. Laura had Shontay's long, warm, naked body clasped hard against hers and her mouth glued heatedly to Shontay's before either of them quite knew what was happening. Shontay responded happily, yielding her mouth, rubbing her body against Laura's, coiling tongues hungrily.

"Only if I can kiss that perfect bottom of yours," Laura whispered to her, letting both hands fall to the wonderful little rump she had admired for months. "I love your little ass. I want your little ass."

"You're going to make me blush, if you don't watch out."

Laura nuzzled her everywhere she could reach with her mouth. "Mmmm, I'm going to make you glow . . . I'm going to make you beg."

Shontay pulled back, almost flirtatiously, batting her eyelashes at Laura, acting faux-coy, twisting her body so that her ass was sticking up, more visible. "You like that bony little thing?"

Now Laura's caresses grew more aggressive. She squeezed one round, spongy-hard little bun with her hand, a delicious, exciting squeeze that made her whole body tingle and made Shontay gasp and instinctively gnaw her lower lip.

"I don't feel any bone there," Laura whispered, eyes flaring. "Just wonderful ass." She slid her fingers into the crack between Shontay's round little buns. "Turn over. Let me kiss that fantastic back of yours too."

With slow, feigned reluctance, Shontay turned onto her stomach, stretching out luxuriously next to Laura, extending the full length of her smooth, supple, slender body, relishing the feeling of Laura's eyes roaming excitedly all over it.

"You are so beautiful . . . how can you hide all this beautiful flesh under those awful suits you wear?" Laura said in an awed, hushed voice, unable to control her renewed lust.

She didn't realize what she had said, about the suits, until it came out of her mouth, but it turned out that Shontay was more thrilled by Laura's enchantment with her naked body than she was hurt by Laura's criticism of her taste in clothes.

"It isn't beautiful. It's skinny," she said, pouting. "And too tall."

That was all Laura needed to unlock the torrents of fresh desire she was feeling, and she immediately straddled the backs of Shontay's thighs and began giving her a slow, sensual back massage. She had earlier thought she could spend a year just kissing this long, smooth brown back anyway, and now she had the chance. She began at the nape of Shontay's neck, truly making love to it and to Shontay's thin shoulders so hungrily that Shontay began shivering and giggling in a soft, sexy voice.

"What's the matter, you don't like the way I dress?" she tried to tease Laura, but very quickly she was panting and even mewling softly as Laura turned up the heat.

Laura kissed her way slowly down the shallow valley formed by Shontay's spine, then back up again, taking constant detours onto the smooth, resilient flesh of the rest of her back, tickling the sensitive nerves under her shoulder blades, which indeed were more prominent than most due to her thin frame. On her second time down the spinal column, Laura's lips arrived at the upward curve of Shontay's sacrum, highlighted on either side by a delicious deep dimple. Oh god, it's perfection! Laura thought, kissing one dimple with carefully controlled but burning adoration, then the other.

Shontay squirmed and whimpered. "God, Laura . . . you're getting me all hot and sticky again. So quick."

Laura's hand dipped between her thin, sleek thighs, finding the small, wet blossom of Shontay's cunt again, while she kissed her way from the second dimple over to the firm, swelling moons of Shontay's small, jutting ass. It was a compact ass, small but beautifully shaped, and she spent the next minutes worshipping it thoroughly with her mouth and her fingers, kneading and squeezing the hard little melons, kissing them, then biting them suggestively, even snarling softly with hungry passion, until Shontay was squirming and whimpering, looking back over her shoulder, grimacing in pleasure, as if fascinated by the sensations Laura was arousing in her perfect little bottom.

Laura's attentions were making Shontay a lot wetter, too. Laura could feel the warm, buttery fluids bathing her fingers as she lightly massaged Shontay's small pussy, reluctant to do it too fast since she didn't want Shontay to come again before she had finished her selfish little feast. By now she knew that Shontay was unlikely to go off unexpectedly, but still she didn't want to risk it. I want to drive her wild, she realized. I want her to claw the sheets and scream. There's only us, nobody can hear us, no Kendra, no Gibsons, except this long, lovely one. Shontay . . . I want you to scream.

"Ohhnnnn!" Shontay moaned, again looking back at Laura, her face contorted in an expression of fierce sexual arousal. "Unhhhhh! Oh *god*, that feels good!"

It's going to feel a lot better than that, darling, Laura thought, beginning to part Shontay's tight little ass cheeks with her fingers and to run the tip of her tongue into the dark, warm crack between them. At first Shontay seemed not to notice, but as Laura's tongue descended further into her crack, she could not help but notice. Her hips shimmied in a sharp, excited spasm, and she tried to twist her body to the side, but Laura was strong and held her steady.

"What . . . are you doing?" Shontay whimpered.

"Mmmm, I'm loving your ass like nobody's ever loved it before," Laura purred.

"Jesus . . . that's what I'm afraid of," Shontay gasped, with a repressed giggle.

"Doesn't it feel good?"

"It feels wonderful!"

The tip of her tongue had finally arrived at Shontay's tight little black rosebud, her ultimate destination, but she already knew it would be too shocking to the girl simply to enter it without warning. Her fingers in Shontay's pussy were all gooey now with warm nectars, and as she slid one up higher into Shontay's crack, she moved her mouth to the side and took a sizable piece of ass-flesh into it, biting it gingerly but firmly.

"Anngghh!" Shontay yelped, distracted enough by the momentary squirt of pleasurable pain not to notice Laura's forefinger sliding up into her anus.

Now Laura peppered the smooth, brown moons with love bites, repeating her first bite everywhere, sucking chunks of firm flesh into her mouth, clamping her teeth on them, burrowing her finger deeper into Shontay's ass at the same time. Shontay mewled and squirmed, but after a few seconds she seemed to know something unusual had happened.

"Oh!" she gasped. "What's that? Unghhhh! Oh . . . Laura," she moaned, her eyes full of hot sex and unanswerable questions as they caught Laura's.

Shontay appeared so shocked that she could not understand where Laura was going with this, but Laura knew very well. Now that she had somewhat loosened the opening, the true rape she had planned was possible.

"Oh, sorry," she winked at Shontay, teasing her, but letting her eyes smoke with sexual threats at the same time.

She extracted her finger from the girl's back track, dropping her hand again to Shontay's dripping pussy. Now she returned her tongue to the wonderfully deep little crack between Shontay's smooth brown buns and, using her free hand to pull them apart, slid the tip of it into the girl's rectum, wriggling it in quickly and as deep as it would go.

"Ahhnnnnneeeee!" Shontay suddenly screamed, though to Laura's ears it was only a hint of the screams she hoped were coming. "Ohhhnnn . . . shit!"

But by now Laura had her in the grip of a thrilling, magnetic sexual rhythm that would not let her go. Now Laura increased the speed of the two fingers she was using to rub Shontay's flowing, throbbing slit, swirling her taut little clit in a hot frenzy now, and driving her tongue deep into the girl's ass. Shontay whooped and clenched her firm little ass cheeks and squirmed, but Laura was aware that she really didn't want to get away, even though the sensations were very intense.

"Oh god . . . what are you doing! God, Laura . . . stop!"

Laura wasn't exactly in a position to discuss it, and in answer she withdrew her tongue temporarily from Shontay's pretty little asshole and began biting her round, swelling, hard buns again, rubbing her pussy even harder and faster.

"Mmmnnggeee!" Shontay squealed, now perceptibly jumping up a notch in tension, so that Laura now knew the girl would come any time. "Oh! Ohnggg!"

"I'm making you come," Laura panted, sinking herself into a passionate depravity that she could barely control. Shontay's long, smooth brown body, though slim, was wildly desirable, especially in this writhing, flexing, quivering state as Shontay approached another orgasm.

"Oh god . . . you're right!" Shontay gasped, dropping her head back to the mattress, even lifting her ass a little to give Laura easier access, swirling it back and up slowly into Laura's face. "Oh god Laura . . . yes! Ungghh! Yes!"

It was a beautiful ass, and Laura worshipped and passion-mauled it at the same time, biting and excitedly pinching the smooth brown moons, now pulling her hand up from Shontay's dripping pussy for a moment to pry both of her buns apart and stab her tongue deep into Shontay's tight little rectum.

"Unggghhh! Oh! Mmmnnggggeee . . . oh . . . Laura! Oh . . . I'm going to—"

Shontay's long, thin body grew suddenly stiff. Laura, her tongue wriggling deep in the girl's moist, clenching asshole, knew she was going to come. Nothing could stop it. Dropping her hand again to

Shontay's streaming pussy, she found Shontay's clit with two fingers and pressed it hard, then rubbed it vigorously, tongue-fucking her ass in a fierce frenzy at the same time.

Shontay's stiffened body suddenly jackknifed up off the bed, a violent, twisting, surging motion that almost dislodged Laura's face from its happy haven between the girl's taut little buns.

"AUUNNGGGGHHNNIIIEEEEEE!" she screamed, collapsing into a mass of shuddering spasms that Laura sustained by continuing to tongue-fuck her ass and rub her pussy. "OHHNNGG! Ungghhhh! Oh . . . shit! Oh Laura . . . auungghhhhh! Nnnggmmmiieeee!"

Her climax seemed about three times more intense than the first one, and about three times longer too. She wailed and screamed and writhed as Laura refused to let her stop, coming, then slumping and panting, then coming again, two full orgasms punctuated by a whole sequence of smaller shocks, until finally she lay gasping and moaning on her stomach, wincing as the last aftershock made her wince and shiver.

Slowly, Laura removed her fingers from Shontay's pussy and her tongue from the girl's pretty little asshole, which she had tongue-raped enthusiastically. Shontay was still trying to regain her breath and her senses. Laura kissed her way up the girl's naked back, now much more tenderly, again brushing away the hair from her neck and kissing the nape sensually.

Shontay stirred and smiled. "You don't give up, do you," she murmured, hoarsely. "I never knew anybody like you."

"Mmmm, I don't know how anybody who could come like that could give up sex," Laura whispered in her ear.

"Are you kidding?" Shontay grinned, rolling over now, facing Laura. "I never came like that in my life. If I had, I probably wouldn't have given it up."

Laura tried to kiss her, but Shontay playfully turned her face away.

"Would you mind rinsing out your mouth before doing that?" she asked. "I love to kiss you, but you just had your tongue in my . . . you know where."

Laura grinned. "Honey, it's clean as a whistle. I just cleaned it out."

"You sure did," Shontay grinned back. She was suddenly gripped by a quick, intense shiver. "See, it makes me almost come again just thinking of it. But do it anyway, okay? Just to make me feel better?"

Making a face, Laura hopped off the bed and went to the bathroom, rinsing out her mouth and returning in seconds.

"I came back for my kiss. It's the least you can give me after coming twice."

Shontay looked very sultry as she welcomed Laura into her arms. "I bet you can too," she purred sexily, much more seductive than Laura had ever dreamed possible. "Twice, I mean. Why don't you stay here tonight? I think I'd be lonely now if you went downstairs. Just stay here, sleep with me, and you can go down and dress before work."

Laura kissed her. "We might not get much sleep."

Shontay looked demurely down, shy and at the same time very excited by what had transpired. "We've got all the rest of our lives to sleep, right?"

***

Laura drifted awake in the morning to the sweet, faintly erotic odors of Shontay's naked flesh pressed against her cheek. It happened to be one of the girl's exquisite, teacup breasts, so round and firm, the nipple so soft and delectable that she could not keep from taking it into her mouth. Shontay stirred and moaned, coming awake. She watched Laura languorously sucking her nipple.

"I never slept with anybody before," she said quietly, stroking the hair away from Laura's forehead. "Like this, I mean." Laura looked at her quizzically, holding Shontay's wet, caramel-colored nipple in her lips. "I always made them go home. Oh, that feels good."

"Mmmm, are you going to make *me* go home?"

Shontay's eyes sparkled with happiness. "You only did it to me about four or five times last night. Don't you ever get tired?"

"Not of 'doing it' to *you*. Do you get tired?"

Shontay shook her head, and they were quickly into another round, making love as if the world outside them no longer existed. At work, Laura was relieved that their duties and responsibilities were entirely separate, and that there was no opportunity for them to meet and betray their sudden intimacy. For the next week, while Shontay's parents were still away, they met each evening for dinner in one or the other apartment, and spent the rest of the night in delicious fucking.

Then she and Shontay had a tender parting on the night before Shontay's parents were due to return. It happened that Laura was scheduled for a conference in Tucson the next day, and they would be apart for the first time in a week.

"Tucson?" Shontay whined.

"Are you going to miss me?"

A big tear was already forming at the bottom of one of Shontay's pale brown eyes. But she sniffled, then wiped it away, all the cold reserve returning to her face.

"Of course not," she said, glaring at Laura. "Why should I miss you?"

"Because nobody can make you come the way I can?" Laura teased.

"Maybe I'll find somebody," Shontay said, with a toss of the head. "Some guys like tall skinny girls."

"Some women like them too," Laura said. "Me, for one."

Now Shontay became pliant, fawn-like. "Will you miss *me*?"

"I'll call you every night."

Why am I saying these things? Laura wondered. She adored Shontay, but she knew she didn't feel the kind of desperate, burning, scorching, searing lust for her that she felt for, say, Deshona. Still, she and Shontay working together had brought Shontay along to a new place, a sexual oasis where she could enjoy a sweet and blissfully intense pleasure that was only possible with Laura. It was hard not to be touched by it, even moved, and Laura gave in without a fight.

"Here's my number," Shontay said, scribbling on the back of her business card. "Don't call me at work. Too dangerous. In fact, we should probably just keep pretending we don't know each other."

What a good idea! Laura thought. Why couldn't I have done that with Randi? Yvette? All the others?

She had actually grown quite fond of Shontay during this week, somehow warmed by Shontay's carefully-masked vulnerability, and her fresh sense of wonder at the sex they shared. No longer was she the cold, calculating, remote bitch Laura had initially thought her to be, the careerist, the haughty tall girl who looked down both physically and socially on everyone. She was instead a delightful young girl who was having several orgasms each day because Laura was wildly infatuated with her as a bed partner.

On the flight to Tucson, Laura even felt pangs of separation from her and was very troubled. Her life was complicated enough, she thought, and screwing her neighbors' daughter could only make it worse. For example, could she and Shontay make love in her, Laura's, apartment when Shontay's parents might be home upstairs? It had been bad enough trying to muffle every stray groan and gasp before with her visitors; what would it be like if Shontay were about to scream in ecstasy? (And Laura had learned how to make her scream, and also whinny uncontrollably.)

The conference was dull but enlivened by Laura unexpectedly running into Lila, and the rest was history. It took a little persuading, as it usually did with the profoundly inhibited Lila, but Laura quickly got her into bed again, and they spent the rest of their few hours at the conference screwing heatedly. Laura forgot to call Shontay, as she had promised she would. She had forgotten about Shontay entirely, and Shontay was not pleased.

On the phone, when Laura finally did get around to calling, she was distant, haughty, querulous, cold by turns, everything Laura had found her to be before their warming—their thrilling, sensitive, and multi-orgasmic nights together in bed in her parents' apartment.

"You said you would call!" she whined at Laura.

"I . . . couldn't," Laura said, truthfully. "I was too tired. The damn dinner went on forever. I'm sorry. I was thinking of you." Liar.

Shontay punished her a few more minutes before softening. Laura had called her at home right after rushing from Lila's room over to her own to change. Her body was still tingling from fucking with Lila only moments earlier. She felt guiltier than ever about lying to Shontay, but there was no choice.

"You'll never guess what I did," Shontay said, softly. "Last night. I was thinking of you at that conference . . . and I did . . . you know, what we did together. The first time. You know . . . by myself. But I was thinking of you. It was the best ever, that way. I miss you, Laura."

Laura was touched, and troubled, at the same time. "I miss you too, darling," she whispered.

"Call me tonight? I could do it while I'm talking to you on the phone. I'll bet that would be fun."

"I promise."

It wasn't easy, but that night she had told Lila she had a mild headache and needed a quick nap. She went to her room, promising to meet Lila in about an hour, and phoned Shontay, who was eagerly awaiting her call. Then, in one of the most exciting phone conversations Laura had experienced in recent years, Shontay brought herself to two orgasms while Laura listened and murmured to her.

She also begged to know that Laura was doing it too, at the same time. Wanting to save herself for Lila later, Laura had complied by moaning and faking it, pretending to come when Shontay's voice on the other end was out of control, gasping and squeaking a little, then sighing, feeling mortified and massively guilty for this deception. Why couldn't I just go ahead and do it? she had wondered.

But Shontay was none the wiser, and their conversation concluded with lengthy very soft murmurings of affection that Laura figured would hold the darling, complex girl for a few days until she got back.

***

She came awake a few days later Laura in Shontay's bed—in Shontay's apartment, too, instead of the Gibsons' place above her own—

but dreaming of Lila. It was a real dream, and guilt or chagrin would have to wait until later. In the dream, Laura was on her back, and Lila was on top of her. Both were naked. Laura could feel Lila's very firm breasts and the thick soft bulbs of her nipples moving against her own skin. Lila slithered her long tongue deep into Laura's mouth. Laura almost came in her sleep, and then slid abruptly into consciousness.

She was face to face with Shontay, who was still in a deep sleep, breathing evenly, looking pure and lovely. When awake, Shontay's face had an habitually cold and arrogant cast, which she had now partially softened due to her fondness for Laura, when they were together. But in sleep she looked as angelic as a child. Her hair, usually pulled back severely, came down for fucking with Laura, and now it was tangled and drooping across her face in stray locks, making her look very sensual and fetching.

They had fucked at first in an insatiable frenzy, spurred on by the memory of Shontay masturbating while Laura listened on the telephone from Tucson. Then they had settled into a more relaxed rhythm, though by midnight both were so exhausted they could barely move. Laura understood why Shontay was zonked. On the other hand, she wondered how she could possibly be so oversexed as to have dreams of fucking with Lila after what she and Shontay had done before falling asleep.

Over Shontay's thin, light brown shoulder she could see the clock on her vanity table. It was six-ten a.m. She had to go to work—so did Shontay, for that matter—and had had no intention of spending the night. Now she would have to drive home, shower, change, and rush to make it on time.

She kissed Shontay's cheek. "Good morning, sunshine," she whispered. "I've got to go home and change for work."

Shontay smiled drowsily, stretching, slowly coming awake. In fact, she could not stop smiling as she gazed into Laura's eyes.

"Did we really do what I think we did last night?" she asked softly.

Laura nodded, kissing her mouth. "I guess it was worth waiting for, right?"

Shontay frowned slightly. "Are you sure I satisfy you? I mean, I can tell you must've had a lot of . . . other girls. It makes me a little . . . jealous . . . and also a little insecure."

Laura gulped. How could she just get up and leave with Shontay feeling like that? Instead, she embraced her, kissed her, rubbed her whole body against Shontay's long, skinny body in a way that made them both remember the previous night in acute detail.

"Darling, you do more than satisfy me," she purred. "You make me shimmer and glow. When I'm away from you, I just dream of the way your lips feel on my pussy."

"Really?" Shontay's high forehead knitted up.

"Really." She brushed the hair away from Shontay's smooth cheek, touched by the girl's innocence. "Do you think of me?"

"All the time. I think mostly of when we did it the first time. I was so scared. You wouldn't believe how scared I was. I give a good imitation of courage, but I'm really scared shitless most of the time."

Laura squeezed her tightly and nibbled her earlobe. "Welcome to the club," she breathed softly into Shontay's ear. "You know . . . I have to go home and change, but I can't seem to make myself let this beautiful body go."

"You mean this skinny, bony, gangly body?"

Now Laura was kissing her the way she had kissed her last night. "I mean this long . . . beautiful . . . slender body," she murmured, kissing

Shontay's upper chest and collarbones and throat, now kneading the girl's charming teacup breasts with her fingers. "I think I suddenly need another one before we stop."

"Oh god, me too! Unhhhhh! Oh . . . Laura . . . yes, I think we have just a little time. Do that again. Please!"

While kissing her throat and her delectably straight collarbones, and fondling her small breasts, Laura had dropped one hand between their bodies and lightly pinched Shontay's small clit, very gently, only enough to give her a happy twinge, but apparently enough to make her blood leap.

Sometimes in the morning, awakening after a night of exhausting sex, Laura felt a surprisingly fresh and insistent flash of lust. Both of them seemed to feel it at this instant, and they kissed hungrily, panting and whimpering.

"Touch me . . . touch me too," Laura panted to Shontay.

Shontay dropped her hand. "Like this?"

"Yes! Oh . . . yes! Unhhh!"

Shontay's pale brown eyes were wide and shiny, locked with Laura's, throbbing. "Oh!" she gasped. Her eyes rolled up.

"Yes . . . yes darling yes oh . . . god yes!"

For the next several seconds they kissed with extra sensuality, intermingling their tongues and their moist breath, their naked breasts brushing and their fingers moving rapidly below, their lower bodies beginning to pitch and roll in unison. The moment approached. They were tightly synchronized, looking into each other's eyes, moaning softly.

"Come with me, baby," Laura panted. "I'm going to . . ."

"Oh Laura . . . oh Laura yes . . . oh Laura! Unhhh! Oh . . . Laura! Oh!"

Shontay's eyes rolled up again, and she began to come. Laura was conscious for only the split second it took her to see this, and then she began to come too, an exquisite, hard, piercing ecstasy that felt almost painful in its intensity, the final one in a long string of orgasms that had started the night before. Her body clenched so hard that it was almost like a charley-horse, and recovering from it left her dazed and speechless.

She could tell by gazing at Shontay's face that Shontay's orgasm had been equally sharp. After the grimace of near-pain faded from her features, Shontay was still stunned and numb.

"Excuse me," she half-coughed, clearing her throat, after a minute or so had elapsed. "That really . . . sort of got to me. It almost hurt, it was so hard."

"Tell me about it," Laura whispered in acknowledgement, tightening her embrace. "For a minute I was paralyzed." She laughed softly and kissed Shontay's gleaming wide forehead, now shiny with a thin film of sweat. "I guess you don't have to worry any more about satisfying me."

Shontay glowed with half-embarrassed pride.

Now that they had patched up things and improved Shontay's confidence, Laura felt more relaxed about hurrying home to dress for work. Coming into her building, she actually ran into Mr. Gibson, Shontay's father, coming down to the lobby to get his morning paper. They exchanged morning pleasantries, but Laura could not ignore the look in his eyes. He clearly thought it very odd, and a little scandalous, that she would be coming in at seven o'clock in the morning, still dressed in yesterday's work clothes, looking a little frazzled and worn. Laura remembered how she and Dawn had nearly raised the roof with their cries and fierce, ecstatic shrieks only a few nights ago; she still had no idea whether the Gibsons had been home to overhear them.

This thought made her blush pretty deeply. Oh, forget it, she told herself. It's none of his business what I do. I'm just a little sleepy and dreamy and tingling all over, she smiled. After a night (and a brief awakening) full of thrilling sex. And with your own daughter, too, Mr. Respectable Gibson. Did you know she likes to suck my pretty pussy? Wouldn't that put frost on your balls?

**

Ever since Laura and Taneesha had run into Shontay in the hallway outside Laura's apartment—a scene so painful to remember that Laura avoided anything but a high-level awareness in her mind that it had indeed happened—Laura had been tormented by her realization that Shontay's feelings for her were somehow deeper than she had known. She kicked herself for not having understood it.

Though at work Shontay was aloof, cold, implacable, and apparently much disliked by her direct reports, with Laura she was soft, vulnerable, pliant, and warm, full of delight in her own body, which before Laura she had apparently come to hate and detest for its long, bony frame and sharp angles, and also her inability to come very easily. Before Laura, she confessed, she had never climaxed with another person—meaning a man, of course—only by masturbating.

Laura had quickly put an end to that, and with her Shontay now had several orgasms each time, some of them stupendous shockers that left her weak and gasping. For Shontay, Laura realized belatedly, it was like being reborn. She had blossomed, at least when she was with Laura. She was relaxed, funny, sensual, and very affectionate. She had even left her old baggy business suits in the closet and began to show off a more stylish wardrobe at work—which Laura, fearing a scene, had only detected by spying around corners—one that more successfully flattered her long, slender legs and charming little rump.

Laura cursed herself for not having seen these signs. Anyone would have noticed them. You might not want to call it 'love,' but it was surely a deep sexual attachment and also a deep affection they shared. For all Laura knew, Shontay did think of it as 'love'. She certainly had seemed startled and pained to see Laura with another woman (or girl, Laura thought; it was hard to think of the delicious 'Valley Girl' Taneesha as a woman, though she fucked like one). Shontay, seeing them, had clearly been devastated. Laura could still see the big, silvery tears sliding silently down her smooth, light brown cheeks, her magical pale brown eyes above them stricken and lost.

For nearly two weeks now at work Laura had played cat-and-mouse, trying to avoid her, coming early, leaving late, skirting the areas where Shontay was certain to be. She wondered if Shontay might not be doing the same thing, since they never ran into one another. But the guilt kept gnawing at her, and then the desire, for she actually missed Shontay. Their intimacy had been unexpected, but Laura found that it was captivating. And the more she recalled Shontay standing in the hallway with tears sliding down her cheeks, the more she felt a deep urge to comfort her, to enfold her, to reassure her (by what, more lies? she wondered), and ultimately to take off her pretty new clothes and rub against her until Shontay exploded in ecstasies even more intense than the ones she had experienced so far.

Laura did not know how to deal with this impasse. Shontay could be frighteningly cold and withering in her personal manner, and Laura realized she was a little afraid of her (probably the reason Shontay's employees feared her, too). She could be cutting. She could be an ice pillar of scorn. And Laura knew she herself deserved whatever was coming her way, which made it harder to invite it.

Trying to turn her thoughts to other things, she contemplated moving to a new place. She had lied about it to Taneesha, but the very process of lying had made her wonder if it might not be a good idea. Maybe it was just a peculiar architectural flaw that made the sounds generated in her apartment so audible in the one above. She never experienced such anxieties at Sara's place, or Deshona's, or

Bonnie's. And god knows, we sure whoop it up sometimes, she thought. It's only in my place that I feel this terrible fear that they're going to hear us shrieking.

She was thinking of this so hard one evening as she came home from work that she barely noticed the Gibsons wheeling their stylish and expensive luggage out the door to their Mercedes as she was checking for her mail. They smiled at her vaguely, and she returned the abstracted, neighborly smile they had all apparently agreed on. Then, as she was looking through her mail before heading for the elevator, it occurred to her that they were leaving . . . for a vacation, or a meeting, or something.

Oh god, does that mean Shontay will be coming back over here to feed the cat? she wondered.

As far as she knew, no one showed up the first night, which was the actual night the Gibsons had left. At least, Laura heard no sounds overhead. Though she usually heard little from them when they were home, occasionally a floorboard would creak, or there would be a distant thump, as if something were dropped. She heard nothing.

This made her all the more nervous on the second evening, because if Shontay were dropping by to feed Willie, she certainly would not wait much longer. And in fact, Laura did hear a noise upstairs on the second evening, a definite creak. She's there! she thought.

Laura took a deep breath. I'm going up there. I'm going to knock on the door. I'm going to . . . what? I'm going to apologize. I'm going to tell her that I wouldn't have hurt her for the world. I'm going to tell her I'm just so sorry . . .

She clenched her fists and gritted her teeth, pacing, all in the effort to get courage, to be honest and forthright, to face up to whatever pain she had caused and try to remedy the situation. Seconds later, before she could think of it anymore and allow herself to back out, she was heading up the stairs next to the elevator. She reached the ninth floor and marched resolutely down to the Gibsons' door and knocked.

Then, as she stood waiting, all her courage suddenly left her, draining away like the water in the bottom of a basin. It quickly dawned on her that Shontay would not open the door since she would know it could only be one of two unpleasant possibilities: either a rapist or burglar had got into the building, or it was Laura.

Her heart almost stopped when she heard a small click inside, behind the door. Then she realized it was the tiny hatch-door on the little peep hole in the middle of the door, about average eye-height. She had one on her own peep hole, since it was the same door. Everything was the same. Why couldn't they just make a stupid hole and leave the little hatch-door off? she wondered, knowing that Shontay—or someone, at least—was inside inspecting her now, looking at her, deciding whether to open the door.

"Shontay . . . it's me," Laura burst out, not having prepared to say anything, just hearing the words rush from her mouth in a hushed but semi-hysterical flood.

Still, nothing. No movement or sound from behind the door. Laura looked directly at the peep hole, composing her face into a soft, smiling, friendly mode. Just dropped by to say hi, her face tried to say. I'm . . . oh, you know, just friendly, neighborly Laura, not trying to . . . force myself on you or anything. Just wanted to talk, that's all. She smiled, then was afraid she had smiled too broadly, too falsely, and so shrunk her smiling muscles a little to appear more formal, more restrained.

Whether this strategy worked, or whether Shontay too found the moment becoming unbearable, the door was unlocked and slowly it opened—just a crack, though. Shontay peered out at Laura, her face expressionless.

"Hello . . . Laura," she said, very softly. Her eyes were intense and unrelenting, holding Laura's, boring into Laura's. "What do you want?"

The silence in the hallway where Laura was standing was painful, like a mausoleum, the place where dead dreams went to repose. Laura twisted her fingers.

"I wanted . . . to talk to you."

"That's all?"

Laura nodded.

"Talk, then."

Laura thought of asking to be invited in, then thought better of it. "I . . . wanted to . . . explain."

"You ain't got nothing to explain to me, girl," Shontay snapped, without, however, raising her voice. Her pale, fantastic, light brown eyes glowed with fierce hostility.

Laura had never heard her lapse into this kind of dialect before, which gave added emphasis to Shontay's controlled fury. No wonder I was afraid of her, Laura thought. Look at how stiff she is . . . and god, she looks magnificent when she's angry, with her regal, fierce contempt, her nostrils twitching like that. Laura fought against the clear realization that it was sexually arousing.

She shrugged, not disguising her feeling of defeat. "I wanted to apologize," she said, softly.

She let her eyes do the pleading, hoping to see some sign of softening in this magnificent, haughty, regal creature whose eyes burned and whose chin was held higher than normal, at an imperious height, which made Laura feel even smaller. Shontay glowered at her.

"Go ahead," she breathed finally, almost inaudibly, as if trying to decide whether to be bored or even angrier. "Apologize."

"Look . . . it's kind of hard to do it just . . . standing here. Could I come in? I won't stay but a minute."

Shontay glowered at her. She pushed the door open further and stepped back. Laura, very tentatively, as if she were going to be sliced and shredded instantly by invisible knives, stepped inside. Nervously glancing around Shontay's tall, angular body, she saw Willie, the cat, in the living room, a blur of white fluff with iridescent turquoise eyes, looking at them both. She brought her eyes—reluctantly, fearing the fiery anger there—back to Shontay's.

But now she saw in them what she had not been able to detect in the dim hallway: the faint, insistent throbbing of a deep and real pain, though it was almost successfully masked by the hideous and threatening anger Laura had initially responded to. But seeing it was, curiously, a relief to her. At least she's human, Laura thought, watching Shontay close the door. She did not fasten the deadbolt lock, clearly expecting a short visit, and also making it clear, in case Laura should be devious enough to have any ideas of reconciliation, that nothing more than stammered apologies would be tolerated.

Shontay did not move. She did not try to draw Laura further into the apartment.

"Go ahead."

"Shontay . . . that girl you saw me with is . . . the niece of a friend of mine, a business associate, actually," Laura began, sounding to herself horribly false and treacly.

Shontay looked at her, expressionless again, and said nothing. The silence propelled Laura forward.

"It was just . . . something that happened. I didn't mean to hurt you."

Shontay nodded, a very slight, menacing up and down movement of her head. Her sensual lips were pressed together in a straight line, her eyes hard.

"You didn't," she said in a clipped voice.

"Oh." Laura paused uncomfortably. "I—"

"Is that all?"

"No, it's not 'all'.

Shontay's pale brown eyes flashed. "I don't have anything more to say to you, Laura."

Laura put a hand on her wrist, instinctively, without really knowing she was doing so. Shontay snatched her hand away.

"Don't you touch me!"

"Shontay . . . for god's sake. Please."

"Go, Laura. Go."

"I don't want to go."

Shontay looked exasperated. "I want you to."

Laura was determined not to leave. There was too much at stake. It could not end like this. She sucked up her courage and took a step forward. She raised her hand to caress Shontay's cheek, as she had done many times in the past. Shontay parried it quickly with her forearm, a slashing movement that pushed Laura's arm awkwardly to the side.

Laura's shoulders slumped. She wasn't willing to fight physically about it. She felt defeated. Willie took this opportunity to show up at the door. He recognized Laura and began rubbing against her ankle. She smiled and looked down at him, hearing him purr loudly.

"At least somebody's happy to see me."

She looked up and saw Shontay's eyes cloud over briefly, a surprise to Laura, and apparently to Shontay too since she immediately turned her head to the side and shook it, as if to clear the cobwebs. Laura quickly leaped on her advantage.

"Shontay . . . I'm not going. Not until we talk."

"You already talked. You said you were sorry. Thank you. Apology accepted."

She tried to step toward the door to open it again, but Laura blocked her way. "No . . . we have to talk more."

Shontay shook her head, her eyes again steely and fierce. Laura did not know what to do but felt something must be done, and so she stepped around her and walked into the living room, sitting down in a large, soft-upholstered easy chair that she had not noticed on her last visit. Maybe it was new. It was very comfortable, and she sank a little into the cushions, suddenly realizing that this was a disadvantageous position for her since she was slumped awkwardly in the soft chair while Shontay now loomed over her, angular and tall and imperious as ever, as she approached.

Laura struggled back up, sitting perched on the edge. But instead of confronting her, Shontay sat on the sofa across from her. Willie came in and stared back and forth at the two of them, as if not knowing which one to approach.

"You've got Willie confused," Laura said, calmly. "He thinks we're fighting. He doesn't know which one to snuggle up to. Last time he saw me we were naked and . . . you know, happy together."

Shontay scowled, as if Laura had said something obscene and loathsome. Don't remind me, her eyes said.

"I really like your new clothes," Laura said, rushing on, unwilling to let Shontay gather her anger for a new assault. "They look so stylish on you. They really show off your best features. I especially like that dress. So summery and . . . you know, bright. The bright colors look great on you."

Shontay really did look terrific, Laura thought. She might be cold and implacable, but physically she looked like a model, thin and beautiful in her bright, flowery dress, which clung around her long, thin, but very shapely legs. The ivory hue of the fabric, which was splashed with brightly colored flowers, was especially striking against Shontay's smooth, light brown skin and made her look a little darker than she really was, like rich, thick molasses.

"Thank you," Shontay swallowed uncomfortably, wary of accepting any compliments from someone as devious and treacherous as Laura. ". . . I guess. You were the one who criticized my clothes, remember?"

She said this without a trace of humor, as if she resented it deeply. And yet she *had* changed her style, and the results were undeniably successful. Laura took this contradictory signal as an encouraging sign. She hates me, but she can't forget. I made her pant.

Laura smiled at her warmly, this time genuinely forgoing all the sentimental treacle she had initially had hoped would break down Shontay's resistance.

"Can't we be friends again?" she asked, softly.

"Who said we're not friends," Shontay said, not smiling, in fact very grim.

Feeling very emboldened but still not knowing if anything would come of it, Laura stood up from the easy chair and went over to the sofa, sitting down cross-legged on the floor next to it, and next to Shontay's legs. She smiled up at Shontay and rubbed her cheek against the skirt of Shontay's summery dress, where its folds fell behind her calf.

"It smells good, too," Laura whispered. "*You* smell good."

"I think you better leave."

"You look so much more beautiful with your hair down. Why don't you take it down? Why don't you let me take it down?"

Shontay shook her head.

They did not speak for several minutes. Laura's brain was working furiously, and she wondered if Shontay's brain were scheming too. Parry . . . thrust . . . parry. Will she give in? Will she give up?

"I was looking through this big coffee table book I have about models," Shontay finally said, quietly, almost inaudibly. "I saw this picture of, what was her name, Stephanie something . . . Seymour. Stephanie Seymour. Do you know her?"

"I've never been introduced," Laura smiled.

"I mean who she is. You look just like her. She was a famous model. Probably still is, but she must be a little older now."

"You're the one who looks like the model," Laura said.

"You mean tall and skinny?" Shontay said, revealing a trace of her old bitterness.

"I mean tall and slender and impossibly beautiful," Laura said, looking up over Shontay's knees and straight into her eyes.

"That's just bullshit, Laura," Shontay said, breathing more than speaking the words. "That girl you were with was beautiful."

The knife turned in Laura's gut. She had thought they were slowly, painfully climbing out of this particular morass, and now they had fallen abruptly back into it. Instead of allowing it to happen, she charged on blithely.

"Maybe all you need is a little more meat and potatoes. Why don't you come downstairs and let me cook you a big dinner. I can cook, you know."

Shontay grinned. "I know. You helped me in the kitchen right here, don't you remember?"

"I do remember." Laura let her eyes flow and crackle with sexual innuendo. "I remember everything."

Shontay looked away. "I'm not hungry."

By this time Willie had found Laura's lap. Laura petted him in a relaxed, leisurely way and again rubbed her cheek sensually against the fabric of Shontay's dress, this time letting her cheek brush also against the smooth, warm skin of Shontay's long, shapely calf. Shontay felt it too. She pulled her leg away, not dramatically, but just far enough to make it clear to Laura what was off limits.

"I'm going to have a cigarette," Shontay said, abruptly pushing herself up from the sofa.

Laura had forgotten that Shontay smoked, especially in tense moments like this. She was a little disconsolate, sitting on the floor with her back to the sofa, petting Willie, feeling foolish. On the other hand, being at floor level gave her the opportunity to stare at Shontay's ravishing long legs as she walked across the room on her way to the kitchen to get a saucer to use for an ashtray. The skirt of her thin, flowery dress fell only to her knees, and her long, willowy, flexing brown calves were fully—gloriously—visible. Laura, as she watched the sleek muscles ripple, could not now hide from herself the distant quivering deep inside her pussy.

She fully expected Shontay to avoid the sofa when she returned, since Laura had so obviously been trying to weaken her by subtle, devious caresses, but instead she came right back with her lit cigarette and saucer to the same spot and sat down. She placed the saucer on the coffee table and expelled two long streams of tobacco smoke from her nostrils. She was nearly as stiff and contemptuous as ever, but Laura wondered if this were a sign.

Where do we go now? she wondered.

She noticed that Shontay's legs were no further away from her than they had been when she stood up, and so she scooted closer to them, readjusting Willie in her lap. She wanted more than anything to kiss one, but instead she leaned across and rubbed her cheek against Shontay's bare calf again, a caress of astonishing intimacy nevertheless, which was not lost on either of them. This time, to Laura's intense delight, Shontay did not move her leg away. Willie, however, probably tired of the maneuvering and the awkward tension between the two women, hopped off Laura's lap and began to preen himself.

Shontay continued to smoke in brusque, haughty movements, blowing smoke out of her mouth now in straight, even streams. Slowly, Laura turned her face, still rubbing her cheek against Shontay's calf muscle, until her lips grazed the girl's hard shin. Shontay didn't move. Laura let her lips slide across the shin bone and over to the curved calf muscle, pressing them lightly against it. Still, Shontay did not move.

Now Laura trailed her fingers tenderly along Shontay's bare leg, caressing it and beginning to kiss Shontay's shapely calf muscle instead of just pressing her lips against it. Now Shontay pulled her leg away, not abruptly, in fact slowly, but with definite intent.

"Don't do that."

She glowered at Laura, her head wreathed in smoked, as Laura looked up at her.

"Your legs are so beautiful," Laura said in a hushed, worshipful voice, meaning every syllable.

"They're skinny. You aren't going to start all that shit again, are you? 'You're legs are so beautiful. You're so gorgeous. Why do you cover up that beautiful body.' Just drop it, okay?"

"Okay."

Laura again scooted closer to the leg Shontay had moved away from her. Next time Shontay moved it, she would truly have to alter her position on the sofa. I'm not going to let you wiggle out of this too easily, darling, Laura thought.

She let a few moments pass, until Shontay had finished her cigarette and snuffed it out in the saucer. When Shontay again sat back, Laura again pressed her cheek against her calf.

"This is getting a little repetitious, Laura," Shontay said, unable to keep a slight trace of amusement out of her voice, but not moving her leg.

"Mmmmm, I'm sorry . . . maybe I should kiss the other one," Laura murmured softly, shifting her position so that she was angled between Shontay's legs, her lips now close to the other smooth, light-molasses colored calf.

She caressed it carefully with both hands and kissed it more ardently, moving her lips up Shontay's shapely calf to her knee, kissing it too. Shontay squirmed a little but did not stop Laura. Her thighs even yawned open slightly as if to help Laura, who obligingly moved her body up a little, planting slow, tender, but increasingly passionate kisses on the smooth inner flesh of Shontay's slender thigh. As her face rose higher, she pushed up the thin skirt of Shontay's dress to about five inches above her knees.

She turned her head and kissed the inner flesh of Shontay's other thigh too, hearing a tiny, half-concealed intake of breath as Shontay gasped. Shontay's delicious thighs were very slim, and Laura could see how she might have been teased by others about them through her no doubt gawky teenaged years: spindleshanks, stilts girl, and other stuff. But now, though thin, they were delightfully firm and shapely, warm and marvelously smooth under Laura's moving lips, the skin richly tan like pale clover honey. Laura, unable to resist, began to lick it sensually, not a major sexual uptick, but just a smooth transition from kissing to also tasting.

A soft, very distant mewling sound came from deep inside Shontay's chest, a sound she tried to conceal by swallowing and breathing more loudly, but she was unsuccessful. She did not move, however, except to open her legs a micro millimeter more for Laura.

Since every time Laura opened her mouth, she got her words flung back in her face, she now kept silent and lavished her attention on kissing Shontay's thighs, which was thrilling her so much anyway that she scarcely had energy for anything else. The feel of Shontay's warm, velvet flesh under her lips was indescribably beautiful and erotic at the same time. The long, smooth muscles of Shontay's thighs tensed, relaxed, flexed in small isolated areas as the sensations caused by Laura's lips excited them, then moved on.

Laura pushed Shontay's skirt up a little farther, moving her face up higher between Shontay's thighs. She could now see the pale green fabric of Shontay's panties in the shadowy valley of her crotch.

"Don't do that," Shontay said, squirming, trying to give her quavering voice an authority that would compel Laura to stop, but not succeeding.

"Don't you like it?" Laura asked softly.

"Yes."

"Then why do you want me to stop?"

"I . . . don't. I hate you, Laura . . . for making me . . . feel this way."

"Mmmm . . . you don't hate me," Laura murmured, her lips moving higher, higher. "You wish I would do this to you every night."

Shontay giggled softly in spite of herself. "Oh god . . . it really feels good," she panted, a trace of a smile now curving the sides of her sensual mouth as she looked down at Laura.

"I'm going to make it feel even better."

"No . . . I don't want you to."

Shontay made of a show of trying to close her legs, to push Laura out, but she was clearly not serious, and Laura gently pushed her thighs open again with her fingers, taking the opportunity to move her lips even higher, so that her mouth was now only inches from Shontay's panties. They were damp, not soggy yet, but noticeably moist, and fragrant with her flowing cunt nectars. Laura knew that Shontay's hot little slit was open and pulsing and oozing behind the thin, damp fabric, and she deliberately—certainly before Shontay had realized that any such move was likely—moved her mouth up farther, pressing her lips into Shontay's pale green panties just where they covered her pussy.

Then she breathed a slow stream of warm air through the fabric directly into Shontay's gaping, aching quim. This caused a deep quiver to roll through Shontay's long body, as if radiating out from the center, where Laura was softly blowing into her pussy through her panties, spreading through her flesh all the way from her toes to her scalp, and she even made a soft whinny as she shook, totally helpless for about three seconds.

"Oh! Don't . . . *do* that!" she gasped. "Ohhhhh!"

Laura ignored her. By now she had pushed the skirt of the flowery dress way up over Shontay's waist, exposing her whole groin. Still pressing her lips against the damp cloth of Shontay's panties, she continued to caress the tense muscles of Shontay's inner thighs with her fingertips, though by now Shontay had begun to squirm so much that gentle caresses were getting to be beside the point. She was whimpering too, though Laura could tell she was embarrassed to have yielded so easily.

"Ohhhnnnn . . . oh Laura . . . what are you doing?"

Laura said nothing. She was still forcing her warm breath through the cloth of Shontay's panties into her wet pussy, and she loved the effect it was having on the girl, who seemed to be turning to jelly before her very eyes, and under her very fingertips. Her warm breath and Shontay's wetness had made the damp cloth sag into the open groove of her pussy, forming a small indentation into which Laura could easily insinuate her tongue.

This she did without hesitation, pushing the cloth into Shontay's pussy and enjoying the tangy dew that now touched her taste buds for the first time. The thick, sweet, musky odors emanating from Shontay's excited cunt became quickly more apparent too, and Shontay stiffened, then undulated, whimpering louder, more aroused than ever.

"Unhhhhh! Oh . . . Laura . . . unnhhhhh! Oh god!"

Having finally got the upperhand, Laura was not about to relent. She did not want to pull back, then have Shontay suddenly regain her self control, shutting her legs, maybe even ordering Laura away. She also knew she had little to fear from Shontay coming too soon, because even though Shontay was clearly aroused, she did not spill over quickly, and in fact Laura was the only one who had been able to make her come, using skill and patience.

And so she worked her tongue deeper, pushing the cloth deeper between Shontay's pussy lips, and feeling the cloth become wetter too against the tip of her tongue, still breathing between Shontay's cunt lips as well as invading them with the rest of her mouth. As her tongue pushed the damp cloth deeper into Shontay's pussy, the edges of Shontay's panties began to pull in, exposing the smooth crease on each side where her thighs joined her pelvis, and also a glistening black fringe of shiny pubic hair on each side.

Laura wondered if she herself could stand the sexual excitement she was creating here. Both she and Shontay had become enveloped very suddenly in a hot cloud of seething sex, and whatever fencing and skittishness they had both displayed earlier had completely vanished. She caressed the smooth parts of Shontay's body that had appeared where her panties had pulled away, pushing the cloth even deeper into the girl's pussy with her tongue, then pressing the flat base of her tongue hard against the top where she knew Shontay's tiny, engorged clit had to be.

"Ungghhhh!" Shontay suddenly groaned.

"Oh yes," Laura heard herself murmuring, thrusting her tongue forward, waggling her head a little, letting Shontay feel the full force against her clit and the upper part of her small pussy through the wet cloth of her panties.

"Unnghhh! Laura!" she groaned again.

Now Laura pulled the wet cloth out of Shontay's pussy with her fingers, tugging it to the side, and allowed her tongue to slip directly between the slick, buttery black lips and into the shiny hot pink cleft. Shontay's body arched against the back of the sofa.

"Ohnngg! Oh shit!"

"Honey . . . honey . . ." Laura purred, slowing the pace a little, now fearing that Shontay might indeed come too quickly after all.

The girl was wildly excited, her mysterious pale brown eyes flecked with dancing sparks of sexual fire as she looked down at Laura's face in her crotch. She was so lovely and vulnerable here with her summery dress pushed up around her waist, her body lying askew across the sofa, her hair half-disheveled and beginning to fray and stick out from its tight bun, her honey golden thighs spread, her mouth slack, her eyes throbbing, her pussy wet and red and swollen, that half of Laura wanted to just go ahead and deliver the *coup de grâce* right now.

She's going to come. She's going to come hard. I can just go ahead and let it happen.

But the other half of her wanted more and had begun to form an idea. She began to pull Shontay's panties down, pushing her yawning thighs shut for a moment to get them down over her knees, then kissing her smooth belly as she pulled them off and cooing to her at the same time.

"Take this off . . ." she cooed softly, working quickly. "We'll just take all this off and . . . get it out of the way . . . yes."

As if sunk in a hypnotic trance, a deep swoon or sexual dream, Shontay moved mechanically to allow Laura to remove her panties, then her dress. Then Laura was out of her own clothes in a flash, pulling Shontay across the room to the large, overstuffed easy chair she herself had been sitting in earlier. She again marveled at Shontay's long—very long—smooth brown back as she leaned forward to unclasp her bra, skimming it off Shontay's shoulders with both hands and planting a kiss between her shoulder blades.

"This way," she coached, turning the girl and sitting her gently down in the chair. "I want you . . . oh Shontay, I want you so bad."

Shontay said nothing, panting softly, looking up at Laura obediently—so different from her usual sharp and imperious manner—as Laura placed her in the chair. Laura pulled the girl's long, angular body forward so that Shontay's perfect little rump was perched on the edge of the seat cushion, the rest of her slender torso leaning back at a forty-five degree angle into the chair. Shontay's small, delicious breasts swirled and jiggled as she settled back, and Laura could not keep herself from caressing them with her fingers, gently kneading Shontay's dark caramel nipples, wanting to suck and swallow them, but saving it for later.

"Oh Laura . . . what are we doing?" Shontay asked in a small, quavering voice, as if she were a small child embarking on a strange adventure.

"This is what we're doing," Laura chuffed, panting herself as she now spread Shontay's long legs, pushing them up and back and propping them over the arms of the chair, exposing the wet, bright pink, inflamed seam of Shontay's glistening pussy.

Her blood was racing so fast that she wondered why it didn't just gush up from her throat, or spurt out from under her fingernails. Her body was raging with hot, happy lust for this long, lovely girl, who had been so cruelly rejecting her only moments earlier. And she could see from the rapid pulsing in Shontay's magical light brown eyes that Shontay was feeling equally hot.

In one graceful motion, Laura, facing Shontay, climbed onto the chair herself, placing the crook of each knee over the chair's arms, pressing the insides of her own thighs against the yawning, uptilted backs of Shontay's sleek light brown thighs, and lowered her own throbbing, oozing pussy onto Shontay's. She grabbed the back of the chair above Shontay's head with both hands to steady herself.

"Ahhhh!" Shontay gasped as she felt Laura's wet, warm, slippery cunt flesh come into direct contact with her own.

"Oooohhhhh . . . oh god, that feels good!" Laura gasped, looking down at her, catching her eyes, letting the hot current of her lust shoot between them, and smiling inwardly as she felt Shontay's lust shoot back and intermingle with her own.

Shontay nodded, mouth open. "Oh yeah. Oh!"

With a curious smile, twisted alluringly with scorching sexuality, Shontay raised her hands to Laura's dangling breasts and began to squeeze them, twirling and pinching Laura's nipples between her thumbs and forefingers, while Laura began slowly to move her wet pussy up and down against the girl's swollen, gaping furrow. They had made love in several different ways, but their cunts had never touched until now, and Shontay's eyes quickly rolled up as the acute sensations swarmed through her body.

"Unnhhhhhh! Oh . . . oh Laura . . . ohnnnn yes!"

Their position in the chair gave Laura a kind of leverage she had never imagined before, and she could actually fuck Shontay, almost the way a man would, or the way she would with a strap-on, pumping and pushing her pussy hard into Shontay's, making Shontay whimper and her eyelids flutter with each thrust.

"Unhhh! Oh yes . . . I love it that way!" she gasped to Laura. "Oh yes, Laura! Unhhhhh!"

"Oh honey . . . I love your beautiful pussy. It feels so good against mine. Oh Shontay . . . you are so lovely. How could you think I wouldn't want you? Oh god, I want you so much!"

"Ungghh!"

"Am I doing it too hard?"

"Ungghh! No . . . oh no . . . unghhhh! You can . . . do it harder! Oh!"

There was hardly any way Laura could prevent herself from doing it harder. She was so swept up by this novel position, by Shontay's pliant and eager acceptance of it—Shontay was now enthusiastically grinding her hips and pushing her pussy up into Laura's increasingly vigorous thrusts—and by Shontay's fingers feverishly pinching her excited nipples that she could barely control the urge to send them both over the edge in a mere instant into an explosive conflagration of fiery coming.

She knew she could do it. They were both wildly aroused by this style of fucking, and Shontay was moaning and undulating under her, while Laura herself was consumed by sharp, relentless lust for the girl, jabbing and mashing her wet pussy into Shontay's, fucking her hard, and fast, with short, powerful thrusts. But she also knew that neither one of them wanted it to be over, not so fast.

"Ohhhhh . . . oh shit it's so good . . . let's slow down for a second," Laura panted.

Shontay, eyes glowing in their murky light brown depths with fierce embers, looking submissively up at her and instinctually let her body slide into the more graceful motion that Laura had adopted to slow them down.

Still holding onto the back of the chair with her hands for balance, Laura slowed the pace to a rocking, slow, delicious, rhythmic grind, arching her back so that she could push her naked breasts into Shontay's face, gasping as the girl's sensual lips chased her nipples. The thick, shiny, chestnut-colored flag of Laura's long hair fell across Shontay, who tossed her head sensually into it, as if luxuriating in the feel of it sliding across her cheeks and her forehead. The warm wet inner flesh of Laura's pussy slid across the slippery, slick, well-lubricated dark pink interior of Shontay's splayed cunt, driving them both into frenzies of sexual pleasure that made a slow, sensual rhythm less and less possible.

"Suck them harder . . ." Laura panted down to Shontay, whose mouth had caught her nipples, first one, then the other, sucking them busily but not hard enough for Laura. "Harder," Laura panted. "Do it harder . . . yes! Unhhhh!"

Shontay complied, sucking a large chunk of Laura's breast into her mouth, and moving her hands down Laura's sides to her hips at the same time, holding Laura's hips and jabbing and grinding her own cunt up faster and harder into Laura's cunt now as she sucked Laura's breast almost savagely. Laura responded by fucking her harder too, jabbing her pussy down into Shontay's, swirling her hips, jabbing again, rubbing the two hot, streaming slits together until she knew beyond doubt that both were going to simply dissolve into flames in a shattering climax in just seconds.

Oh, you're not going to have any trouble coming this time, honey, Laura thought, as she whipped them both into a keening, whimpering frenzy, fucking Shontay's pussy so hard with her own that the huge easy chair began to rock and move on the carpet. And, as if reading Laura's thoughts, Shontay began to churn and moan rapidly, in an urgent delirium of hot need, grunting softly, almost hysterically as Laura's wet nipple slipped from her mouth.

"I . . . don't know about . . . you . . ." Laura panted heavily, now ramming and rubbing Shontay's pussy roughly with her own, "but I'm . . . going to . . . come. Oh god!"

"Oh yes . . . Laura!" Shontay mewled, her head suddenly jerking to the side and her body buckling under Laura, grimacing, as if a stabbing jolt of fierce pleasure had ripped through her. "Ungghhh!"

Gripping the back of the chair in a purple passion of intense lust, Laura jammed her wet pussy into Shontay's, giving the girl several short, quick, hard, fierce rabbit jabs, bringing them both to a shockingly explosive orgasm at nearly the same instant. Actually, Laura was lucky this time since Shontay came a few seconds before she did, in contrast to the way it usually happened.

Usually Laura tried and tried to hold off but spilled over just before Shontay arrived at the finish line, which was not so bad seeing as how they both just collapsed in convulsions together. But this time, even while surging and whimpering and panting in the grip of her own sharp and urgent lust, she realized that Shontay had beat her there and was already in the grasp of an orgasmic seizure that had wrenched the breath from her body.

"Ahhnnnn . . . ahhnnnnn!" Shontay moaned helplessly under Laura in the chair.

"Oh . . . now!" Laura gasped, almost unable to get the words out reflexively as she felt sharp contractions begin deep inside her own body.

"Unnngghgh!   Oh   Laura!   Anngghhiieeeee! Unnmmmgghaaiiiee!" Shontay wailed, suddenly stiffening, almost levitating off the chair, pushing her jerking, gyrating pelvis up into Laura's swirling groin, pushing her pussy even harder into Laura's as she came in wild, straining undulations.

"Oh yes . . . oh yes!" Laura gasped, feeling the forcible upsurge of her own climax suddenly stun her from within. "Ahhnngggg! Oh! Ummnnnghaaaiiiii!   Oh shit . . . honey . . . honey!" she keened desperately, sagging down into Shontay, her body shuddering in huge convulsions as a killing orgasm shook her.

It was by far the most tumultuous, thrilling, scorching, and exhausting sexual moment they had ever shared, and Laura instinctively knew as she lay slumped and panting on top of Shontay in the chair that it had altered their relationship in ways they would not understand quickly. Shontay too was stunned and panting, her long, angular body crumpled awkwardly under Laura's, her legs still pinned up and back by Laura's thighs.

"Oh god . . . let me get off of you . . . you'll get a cramp or something," Laura finally said in a hushed, awed voice, as she crawled off the chair and helped Shontay to an upright position.

She could hardly believe what they had done, and the way they had both come so explosively. Somehow from the moment she had pushed the cloth of Shontay's panties up into Shontay's oozing pussy with her tongue, Laura realized that they had both been enveloped in a hot, swirling haze of sex so potent and magical that it had swept them with relentless forward motion to this moment of tingling afterglow and wonder. She could see that Shontay too was only now regaining her senses.

"Wow . . ." Shontay sighed softly, her pale brown eyes widening as she looked into Laura's eyes, her hair spritzing out from all sides, making her look fetchingly soft and mussed and sexy. "That must be what it feels like to get raped."

Even though both of them knew that rape was a bad thing, Shontay didn't look like she felt that a bad thing had been done to her. Quite the opposite.

Laura leaned forward and kissed her high, shiny forehead, gleaming from a thin film of sweat that they had both developed in the heat of this coupling.

"I didn't rape you," she murmured softly, caressing Shontay's cheek as she kissed her. "I fucked you . . . I was wild to fuck you . . . I couldn't stop myself."

Shontay smiled slyly. "I call it rape. And right here in my Daddy's own chair, too."

Laura embraced her, crouching on the floor in front of the chair, leaning forward and up to clasp her awkwardly, but unable to control the urge to hug her hard, luxuriating in the feel of their naked breasts finally mashing together.

"Do you think he'd be upset?" she asked. "Knowing his little girl was being fucked by a raving sex fiend . . . and a woman too . . . and a white woman . . . in his very own easy chair?"

Shontay smiled dreamily, caressing Laura's back with her long, graceful fingers. "What he doesn't know won't hurt him. I'll tell you one thing, though. I'll never be able to look at this chair in the same way again."

Laura laughed softly. Shontay nibbled her ear. It was an awkward position, though, and so she pulled Shontay back to the sofa, where they could spread out and embrace more comfortably.

"Why do you think it matters that you're white?" Shontay asked, seriously.

Laura considered it. "I guess it doesn't. I wondered if maybe it mattered to you."

Shontay looked thoughtful. "I can't say I would have ever done this with a sister, that's true," she said, reflectively.

Laura caressed her perfect collarbones with a fingertip. "You weren't really falling all over yourself to do it with me, either." She nuzzled her long brown neck. "You have the neck of a goddess."

Shontay squirmed restlessly and pulled slightly away from Laura, just enough to look her in the eyes, still very serious. Laura remembered that she had missed the signs before, the signs that Shontay had deeper feelings than she, Laura, had anticipated. She now knew to pay closer attention.

"It wasn't exactly that," Shontay said solemnly. "I was . . . afraid. I could feel myself . . . liking you. I had a couple of white girlfriends in college . . . high school, too. But not really close. We didn't really share much. And when you were up here with me, in the kitchen, I began to feel this . . . I don't know, electricity? This magnetism? And you know, the fact that you were white made it even more . . . how should I say this, mysterious? Exciting?" She raised a hand to Laura's large mane of chestnut hair. "And I wanted to touch your hair. I didn't really think about going any farther than that. Just your hair. But then I saw your eyes looking at me like . . ."

"Like this?" Laura smiled, feeling a sudden influx of renewed desire.

Shontay nodded, half-embarrassed. "Like you wanted to—"

"Fuck you?"

Shontay nodded again. "You always get me . . . with that word. We just don't use that word in my family. My parents, you know, are college professors. My mother teaches at Golden Gate, and my father is in charge of the Institute for Governmental Relations over in Berkeley. That's why they're gone . . . they went to some conference. They're always going to conferences and academic meetings. Anyway, I was brought up to . . . well, just not to use words like that."

"Should I stop using them?"

"God, it makes me so hot when you say it to me," Shontay confessed, breaking into a broad grin.

Without replying, but giving her significant look, Laura now dropped her mouth to Shontay's delicious small breasts. They were the prettiest little teacup-shaped balls of flesh, so small that when Shontay was dressed you doubted they were there. But they were perfect, capped with smallish, dark caramel colored nipples that Laura licked lovingly, slowly, sensually, while Shontay looked down at her.

"You really like them, don't you?" Shontay asked, as if unable to believe it.

This, Laura knew, was actually bait, for Shontay knew how exquisite her breasts were, and that no one would expect to find these rare beauties on such a skinny, tall girl. Laura took one small breast in both hands and sucked the entire globe into her mouth, feeling Shontay's stiffening nipple rub up against the back of her throat.

"Unhhhh!" Shontay moaned. "God, I love it when you do that!"

"Mmmm, I think we're going to end up fucking again, darling," Laura murmured to her, shifting her mouth to the other breast.

Shontay pushed her back again, before Laura could get the second breast entirely into her mouth.

"I want to . . ." she broke up in soft giggles. Then she leaned close, her wet nipples brushing against Laura's breasts, and brought her mouth up to Laura's ear, smoothing aside a large soft curtain of Laura's hair. " . . . to 'fuck' *you* this time."

"Oooohhhhh!" Laura dissolved into giggles of her own, feeling a sharp shiver of excitement that was very apparent to Shontay. "God, I can't wait. In the chair too?"

Now Shontay looked uncertain. "I was thinking of right here."

"Why not the chair?" Laura said, already sliding off the sofa and pulling Shontay with her. "Then, every time you look at it, you'll think of how we both fucked each other into the screaming meemies in it."

Shontay beamed, her tiny breasts bouncing as she followed Laura quickly. Laura turned and sank into the chair, pulling her legs up over the arms, very familiar by now with the position in which she had earlier placed Shontay. But Shontay frowned and pulled her up.

"Not so fast," she complained. "I wasn't finished kissing. I don't want to just . . . you know, fuck. I like it when we sort of . . . go slowly into it."

Laura smiled warmly. "That makes two of us," she said softly, uptilting her mouth to Shontay's.

"You're a good kisser," Shontay murmured after a minute or two of sweet, sensual tongue-intermingling.

Laura again leaned back into the chair, pulling Shontay forward on top of her, embracing her, kissing her more feverishly.

"So are you. I love the feel of your naked body against mine. I want you to fuck me so bad," she breathed into Shontay's mouth, their lips searching each other, their tongues now dancing and stabbing each other. "I want you to fuck me. Please fuck me."

Shontay was starry-eyed; there was no other way to describe it. Her eyes shone with happiness. Laura reached up.

"Only one thing I insist on," she whispered. "Take this hair down. I love it when it falls all around your face. It makes you look so sexy."

"Really?"

Shontay still had trouble sometimes believing she could be sexy. She and Laura hurriedly unfastened the pins that held her hair in place, and Shontay shook it loose. It fell in soft, dark clumps around her cheeks, and just seeing it frame her glowing, happy face seemed to ratchet up the reawakened lust in Laura's pussy a few more notches. God, she is really lovely, she has no idea how lovely she is.

Again Laura scooted back and lifted her body into position on the chair, spreading her thighs wide, watching Shontay's eyes dart to her now-gaping pussy, all slick and wet with fresh, aromatic juice. Yes, honey . . . yes, honey . . . do you want my pussy? Laura said with her eyes. Do you want it? You can have it. Take my pussy . . . honey, take it, take my pussy.

"Come on, you sexy devil," she teased Shontay in a low, smoking voice. "Come here and take what you want from me."

Shontay's sexy smirk grew more serious and dangerous, a change that sent a sexual charge through Laura, making her quiver excitedly inside. Shontay climbed carefully onto the arms of the chair, draping her incredibly long legs over each one, then shifting forward to bring her own pussy close to Laura's. Laura looked up at her, seizing her eyes, forcing Shontay to look deep into her own.

"Oh god, I love the feel of your pussy against mine," Laura panted.

Shontay briefly bit her full lower lip, her pale brown eyes glazing over. "Me too."

She reached forward for the top of the chair back, as Laura had done earlier, both for support and for leverage, and then brought her groin forward until her wet, warm furrow pressed firmly into Laura's. Again Laura quivered throughout her entire body. She marveled that one could feel this sensation twice in one day, relishing the hot, wet, slippery flesh of Shontay's small pussy sliding against the aching, exposed, slick inner folds of her own cunt.

She began swirling her pelvis up into Shontay even before Shontay began any motion herself. For a brief moment Shontay seemed paralyzed, or suspended in a deep, motionless trance of sexual rapture, her cunt glued to Laura's, her whole body locked in a shocking spell of intense pleasure. But then she slowly began to come back to life, swirling her hips too in slow motion with Laura, and even jabbing her pelvis forward now, as Laura had done to her earlier, and as she had told Laura she wanted to do.

"Yes!" Laura panted softly, looking up at her, watching Shontay's small, lovely breasts slide up and down her body as she slowly pumped and gyrated, running her fingers feverishly up and down

Shontay's flexing thighs, and then her long, impossibly long, smooth back. "Ohhnnnngg! Yes! Ohhnnngg yes honey . . . yes honey!"

They kept it up in a slow, grinding rhythm for a few minutes, but Laura grew dismayed as she realized she was going to climax very soon. It rarely took her very long, especially when the situation was as emotionally charged as this one, and the novel position, as well as Shontay's eagerness to be on top, combined to unleash a sharply urgent sexual response in Laura, who began whimpering and bucking under Shontay's thrusting hips, writhing in the large, soft chair, going truly wild.

"Oh! Oh!" she cried out softly, feeling herself lose control. "Oh yes, honey! Oh god . . . do it harder! Ungghhh! Yes! Ungghhh! Yes . . . that's it! Oh, I'm going to come, honey! Fuck me . . .yes . . . fuck me! Just like that . . . ungghhh! Ungghh!"

She knew the words would inflame Shontay, and they had the desired effect. Shontay was breathing hard now too but did not yet seem close to an orgasm, as Laura was. It was always a little harder for her, and Laura knew she should slow down, regain control, take it easy, bring Shontay along with her, let her concentrate instead of distracting her by lots of wild groaning and whimpering. But the words did goad Shontay into a rougher motion, and she began ramming her pussy into Laura's, and rubbing it hard up and down in the splayed crease of Laura's streaming cunt, grinding her lean, angular body down into Laura's uptilting groin, until there was absolutely no way Laura could keep the floods back.

Her body was gripped by a deep, unexpected shudder, which Shontay perceived. She paused for a micro-second, realizing that Laura was coming, then gripped the back of the chair even harder and began pumping Laura in quick, sharp jabs.

"You're . . . coming, aren't you . . . Laura?" she panted, fucking Laura very aggressively now, her long, sharp-angled body releasing a fierce, muscular power Laura had never felt until this moment.

"Ohhhh god yes!" Laura wailed, feeling the preliminary quakes of a stupendous orgasm beginning deep in her belly.

She could actually feel the slippery wet cunt honey that lubricated their two hot pussies increasing, flooding their groins, as they pushed and ground them passionately together. But it was the last surface sensation she experienced before a huge, wrenching spasm seemed to turn her inside out.

"Auunngghhhh!" she groaned, her back arching, bowing upward. "Ungghhmmnniiieeee! Oh! Unmmnnggghiiieee!"

This orgasm was much more severe and shattering than her previous one, and it seemed to rip through her flesh like a spray of red-hot nails, searing her, leaving her breathless, a whimpering mass of tingling flesh under Shontay's slowing thrusts. Laura did not know how long she was throttled and squeezed by this piercing ecstasy, but she came back to her senses to find Shontay still slowly rubbing their pussies together, not making any desperate attempt to get there herself, and realized something was wrong.

She didn't come, poor darling, she thought. She needs to come too. I just stole the show from her, that's all. Effortlessly, Laura slipped down sliding off the seat cushion of the chair but still holding Shontay in place by gently clasping the girl's narrow hips in her hands. This way she could sit on the floor with her head tilted back on the cushion, and Shontay's pretty, small, runny, puckered pussy was poised just above her mouth.

"Oh! Ohhhhh . . . Laura!" Shontay gasped, looking down, as Laura slid her tongue up between the glistening, swollen inner lips. "Unhhhh!"

She threw her head back, and her body tensed up. She's close, Laura realized. Why didn't she go for it? We could've come together, at the same time, I'll bet. Well, never mind, you're going to come now, sweetie. Hold on.

The position they were in suddenly thrilled Laura doubly when she realized she could hold Shontay's beautiful little hard round rump in both hands while she hastily and hungrily devoured the girl's streaming slit. She cupped both perfect little buns in her palms, digging her fingers into the spongy round flesh, eagerly sucking Shontay's cunt lips into her mouth, then slurping and stabbing her open slit passionately with her tongue.

It took only seconds for Shontay to lose control. She began fucking Laura's mouth with her pussy the same way she had moments ago been fucking Laura's cunt with it, grinding her wet quim down into Laura's mouth, whinnying softly as Laura's tongue slid up as far as Laura could make it go inside of her.

"Ohhngggg! Oh god! Oh . . . oh Laura oh god oh yes unnhhhhh!"

Laura had fucked her enough to know that she sometimes had trouble getting there, but she was there now. She grasped Shontay's hard little buttocks fiercely in her hands and sucked as much of Shontay's small cunt as she could into her mouth, especially Shontay's clit, flicking it maniacally with her tongue, feeling the deep shudders begin inside the girl's long, straining body. Holding the back of the chair, which was now rocking and moving again under her thrashing, pumping body, Shontay jammed her throbbing cunt down into Laura's mouth and erupted in a shocking uprush of intense spasms.

"Ohhngghhmmnnnaauuhgghhh!" she cried out, a long, loud wail of almost unbearable rapture that filled the room and Laura's happy ears. "Ungghh! Oh! Auunngghiiiieeeee! Oh shit . . . Laura . . ." she gasped, falling forward, her hands slipping off the top of the chair as she crumpled into an awkward heap slightly above Laura.

She dipped into a brief respite, but Laura sucked her again, squeezing her wonderful spongy cheeks, and quickly brought on another wave.

"Auungghhhhh! Oh . . . god! Oh please . . . oh Laura oh please . . . auungghhhhh! Oh yes!" Shontay whimpered, spilling over again with either the second wave of her orgasm, or with a fresh one.

Laura, smiling, could feel the pussy juices running down her chin, smearing her lips, and she wondered if she had ever been so happy to make another woman come. Certainly not happier. Letting Shontay wind down slowly, but fearing she might cramp somehow if left in this awkward position, Laura carefully extricated herself first and then gently helped Shontay to turn and sink into the soft cushions of the chair.

For several minutes neither of them could speak, following the intense physical and emotional aftermath of this heated collision. It was so still in the Gibsons' apartment that Laura could finally hear their soft breathing. They had stunned one another into silence. Shontay broke it after a few minutes, speaking so softly that Laura could barely hear her.

"I never met anybody at all like you," she said, shaking her head, the hint of a smile curling the corners of her mouth. "I . . . was determined not to talk to you. Ever again. I just wanted to forget it."

Laura, still naked as a jaybird, was sitting with her knees drawn up on the floor at the foot of the chair, her lips only inches from one of Shontay's long, slender, shapely brown legs. She leaned forward and kissed it sensually.

"How could you ever forget it?" she whispered.

Shontay continued shaking her head in disbelief. "I couldn't, I guess. I just wake up every morning wanting you to do that to me. I know . . ." she looked away, embarrassed, "you didn't learn how to do that by yourself. But when I saw you with her—"

Shontay's eyes clouded up briefly, and she looked away. Laura, rising up herself, took her hand and pulled her up out of the chair.

"Come over here again and cuddle with me," she said, drawing Shontay back to the sofa.

Shontay giggled and wiped away a minor tear. "This is where we started," she laughed. "Before we went to the chair. It's starting all over again."

"I promise to behave." They snuggled and nuzzled each other. "Why didn't you come with me . . . I mean, when you got me going like that?" Laura whispered, stroking her pretty little naked ass.

"I don't know. I think maybe I was just so astonished by the way you just . . . went off. So quick. And I was enjoying the feel of it. And I kind of . . . missed the moment, I guess." She smiled and kissed Laura's mouth very emotionally. "But it was all worth it because of what happened next."

"You raped my pussy and my mouth. God, it was wonderful. Let's do it again."

"Could we fix something to eat first? All this . . . 'fucking' . . . makes me kind of hungry."

Shontay looked like she was going to blush. She was demure, coy, flirtatious. Laura had never seen her quite like this. She got to her feet and pulled Shontay up off the sofa, embracing her long, naked body, tilting her head up to kiss her again.

"You are very tall," she said. "My mouth is closer to your breasts than it is to your mouth, unless I stand on my tippy toes."

Shontay smirked. "You can kiss them too," she breathed. "Whenever you want to."

Laura considered it. "Come with me. I'm going to take you downstairs like I promised and feed you some meat and potatoes. I've got two New York strip steaks just waiting for us."

"Two? Were you expecting someone?"

Laura almost laughed. Here they both were stark naked, standing in the middle of Shontay's parents' apartment, having just fucked one another silly twice in her Daddy's easy chair, sparring about food and Laura's other lovers.

"I bought them on the way home," Laura said with a stern face. "I always buy two and freeze one. I just haven't popped it in the freezer yet. What . . . are you refusing free food?"

Wide-eyed and solemn, Shontay shook her head. "I wouldn't think of it. Can I feed Willie first?"

They spotted Willie by the fireplace, looking at them as if they were aliens from another planet.

"I think we might have scared him," Laura said.

"If you ask me, he's getting used to it," Shontay said, sassily. "Every time you appear, we wind up getting naked and moaning and screaming."

"Mmmm," Laura teased her, "maybe he likes the looks of you naked. I sure do."

"Don't be nasty," Shontay smirked. She reached down and retrieved some of her clothes and some of Laura's. "Cover up. I think he likes *you* better. It's all that hair that's got him."

Laura pinned her against the wall again before they left the Gibsons' apartment. She kissed Shontay's neck and ran one hand up her thigh, under her dress, to her ass, squeezing one firm round cheek through her panties.

"I may not let you get away without . . . you know what," she murmured. "You drive me wild with desire."

Shontay trembled but summoned up enough of her old steel for a sharp reply. "Careful what you wish for, girl," she breathed.

The End

Here is a sample from another story you may enjoy:

Hot Lesbian Erotica

Catfight, Climax, Friends Again

by. Miranda Mars

Laura heard something upstairs.

She knew the Gibsons were gone since she had seen them out the window as they were leaving earlier that day, getting into an airport shuttle with several pieces of luggage. That could mean only one thing: Shontay. When her folks were gone, she came over to feed their cat Willie and spend a little time with him. She was up there. She should've taken off her shoes, if she didn't want me to hear her, Laura thought. Maybe she doesn't realize how these old apartments telegraph every little thing.

Shontay still had not phoned Laura. Let's see, it must be almost ten days or so since she called, Laura thought, counting back. Very odd. Something's going on. I bet they told her about the screaming and groaning down here, she thought glumly.

Laura had been in such a flutter of love and exuberant sexual happiness following her night with Sara that almost nothing else had got her attention for days. On top of that, she had engaged a real estate person—a friend of Rhonda's—who had within days found her a delightful condo nestled in a forested slope on the western side of the lower Twin Peaks area. It was heavily wooded and could be foggy at times, but it was fairly new, only one previous owner, and secure and private.

Laura had made it clear to the agent that, as she had put it, she couldn't bear listening to other people's noises, dogs, odious rock music, quarrels, and that that was the reason she was moving in the first place. They performed, with the cooperation of Laura's potential neighbors, several experiments to detect how soundproof these condos were, and Laura was tickled to find that someone playing heavy metal at an ear-shattering volume directly next door might as well be on the moon.

"You could commit murder in here and never be discovered until the smells started emanating," the real estate guy, a dour old man with a huge distended belly and rheumy yellow eyes, said to her, winking.

"No murders," Laura winked back. Even though he was sort of grotesque, she liked him. In fact, she loved him for finding this condo. "I meditate a lot, though. And do my yoga." It was so much fun to make up outlandish stories for strangers.

Her instant offer had been accepted, and the deal was already in escrow. As she looked around her Russian Hill apartment, especially at the view from the windows while sitting in the white sofa (where I've devoured so many lovely girls, she reflected, feeling her pussy tingle happily at the memory), she felt a little sad. You could see the Bay Bridge, and the fog swooping and swirling in over San Francisco Bay. The lights winked on everywhere, and you could even see Berkeley across the Bay when there was no fog. To the left was El Cerrito, where Jane and Kendra were now living. To the right was Oakland, where April lived. Where she's probably churning and groaning on top of that delicious Yolanda at this very moment, Laura thought, enviously. Yolanda is April's new girlfriend. Everybody needed a girlfriend.

The apartment had memories. Most of them were almost unbearably sweet. She would hate to leave it, but one had to move on. It would be such bliss to be able to relax in bed with Sara, say, in her new condo, and do whatever they liked without fear of eavesdropping. The thought of Sara brought her full circle to her obsession of the past few days, since she could not shake Sara out of her mind now, or the memory of Sara's caresses from her body either, or her funny faces, or her big soft black nipples, or her twinkling little silvery pussy ring.

And then she heard another very faint noise from upstairs and realized that Shontay was still there. And avoiding me, she thought. Since they had become lovers, Shontay would always ring Laura's buzzer whenever she came by to feed Willie, if her parents were traveling. But not tonight.

If you enjoyed this sample, then look for **Catfight, Climax, Friends Again.**

Also by this Author:

Deep Excavation

Chocolate Sandwich

Post-Game Specials

A Breach in the Preacher's Daughter

Deeply Detoured

The Rich Bitch Itch

"Hard" Competition

Little Rich Girls Go First

Superior Playmate

Spicing Up a Business Conference

Green Minds Lead to Colorful Results

Dirty Acquaintance

Menage a Trois

Provisional Test

Holiday Treat and Heat

Sex on the 46th Floor

Sneak, Peek and Squeak

Distance Leads to a Sexual Marathon

Confessions and Steamy Clinches

Screams of Pleasure

From the Author

If you'd like to give me comments or suggestions to any of my books, feel free to shoot me an email at:
miranda_mars@awesomeauthors.org.

Check my page on Amazon and my blog for Updates and interesting info.

Author Central - http://amzn.to/14wSFHW
Author Blog - http://miranda-mars.awesomeauthors.org/

If you enjoyed any of my books then please share the love and click like on my books in Amazon.

If you write me a review and send me an email I will send you a free book, or many.
(Just know that these emails are filtered by my publisher.)

Good news is always welcome.

One Last Thing, For Kindle Readers...

When you turn the page, Kindle will give you the opportunity to rate this book and share your thoughts on Facebook and Twitter. If you enjoyed my writings, would you please take a few seconds to let your friends know about it? Because... when they enjoy they will be grateful to you and so will I.

Thank You!

Miranda Mars
Miranda_mars@awesomeauthors.org

About the Author

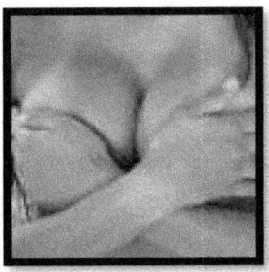

Miranda Mars lives with her cats and her exercise machines with her "special" friend in a suburb in San Francisco. Here is where she lavishly spends scribbling erotica for your, and her own, amusement.

She is especially attracted to dark-skinned women, and uses them as the lovers of the main characters in the stories she writes. She says they're just so hot! So dark-skinned women, BEWARE! :-)

Her stories are also surprisingly VERY ENTERTAINING for MEN!